NOT SO STRAIGHT UP

BOOK TWO

SPIRIT OF HOPS SERIES

J. E. JOYCE

Not So Straight Up

SPIRIT OF HOPS SERIES · BOOK TWO

J.E. JOYCE

Welcome to Rapids Bay Minnesota, where the Viking blood runs strong, secrets don't last long, and the best place to kick back is The Spirit of Hops Brewstillery. Half brewery, half distillery, all hometown watering hole goodness fit for the Gods.

Charlie

Life's too short. Cliché? Yes, but some things are universal truths regardless of how many pumpkin spice-toting basic white girls paint said truths on barn wood and hang them in their kitchens. That basic truth has been my motto for most of my life and has rarely steered me wrong. It may have also steered me into some interesting shenanigans and awkward situations, but those just make for the best stories. As the bar manager for Spirit of Hops Brewstillery in my hometown, those stories have always given me something to chat about with customers. But when the new brewer and his little girl show up, those stories seem just a prologue to the newest adventure I hear calling my name. Life's too short, why not seize the day and see what comes, right?

Callum

If there is one thing I have learned in these last six years watching my little girl grow up, it's that a year is both somehow forever and gone in an instant. Life is too short, and that's not something to be taken lightly. Moving to Rapids Bay, MN to take over as a brewer for Spirit of Hops was the right move for us. I needed a fresh start, my daughter needed a chance to grow up without ghosts of the past, and we both needed a change in scenery. Georgie and Work, that's my world and in that order. But life doesn't like the best-laid plans and when opportunity literally comes crashing into you, you have to take a chance, right?

*For my brewery boys. You know who you are and what you did,
and this book is all your fault.*

# WHISKEER SMASH

- 2 tbsp clear honey
- ½ lemon, diced, plus 2 pared strips of lemon zest, to garnish
- 4 sprigs of rosemary
- 100ml whisky (something smoky works well)

Mix together the honey and 1 tablespoon of boiling water in a cocktail shaker or jar with a lid.

Using a spoon, or the end of a rolling pan, muddle (crush together) the diced lemon and leaves from 2 sprigs of rosemary with the honey mixture.

Add the whisky and shake to combine.

Strain into tumblers filled with lots of crushed ice.

Garnish each glass with a scorched rosemary sprig (use a blowtorch, or the burner on a gas hob, to torch the ends so they release their aromatics), and the lemon zest.

———

PROLOGUE

CALLUM

*A*fter hours of nothing but corn fields and plains grasses, the welcome sign for our new hometown, Rapids Bay, Minnesota is a welcome sight. My six-year-old daughter, Georgie, sits in the backseat of my old but trusty Subaru WRX, her tiny voice filling the air with her special brand of off-key singing and laughter.

"Sing it again, Daddy!" she exclaims, her laughter infectious even after hours trapped in the car. I oblige, hitting a button on my steering wheel to start the song over again for the umpteenth time today. With a deep breath, we both launch into yet another rendition of 'Into the Unknown' from Frozen. While I can feel a migraine building, and my throat may be getting a little sore, I will gladly sing as many songs as she wants. That little girl has me firmly wrapped around her little finger, and she knows it.

As I sing along with Georgie's favorite song of the moment, my thoughts turn to the move, a weirdly profound mood settling over me as we crest a small hill and can see the whole town spreading out before us. I glance in the rearview mirror, smiling at Georgie's beaming face. Her wide blue eyes twinkle with excitement as she clutches her favorite stuffed animal, a little lion. Her blonde curls bounce with every note she sings, and I can't help but smile. This, right here, is why I decided to start fresh in this quaint little town, states away from anything or anyone we know.

Bracing myself against the wave of nerves I feel creeping in, I roll down the window, pull up to a stop sign at the top of the hill, and take a deep breath. The heavy, warm late summer air carries the scent of pine, fresh-cut grass, and something new and fresh.

Rapids Bay is just as picturesque as I had hoped from my quick google session - rows of charming houses with quaint front yard gardens overflowing with late summer flowers, a bustling main street lined with local shops, and a serene view of the river that winds its way through the heart of it all. It's a far cry from the hustle and bustle of Denver, where we came from. As I look around, a buzz of excitement settles over me in a way I haven't let myself feel until now.

At thirty-four, I'm not exactly old, but I sure as hell don't feel young either. My days of reckless abandon are long gone, replaced by the sobering responsibilities of fatherhood. Before Georgie came into my life, I wouldn't have thought twice about packing everything up and moving halfway across the country to try out a new job. Hell, I had done precisely that more than once since college. But now, with my daughter to consider, I can't help questioning my every action and wondering if this move was best for us.

I glance down at my phone, rechecking the GPS to see where I am supposed to turn to get to the apartment building. The music app is up on my screen instead of the map like I was expecting, so I quickly swipe back to navigate to the map. Georgie's song keeps playing through the car, her tiny, enthusiastic voice ringing over the recording as mine fades and my concentration turns to my phone. The map finally loads, and I watch as the GPS recalculates.

A SUDDEN, sharp crunch shatters the tight hold on the peace I've been clinging to the last few days. The car jolts forward, and I grip the steering wheel, my heart racing. I glance at Georgie in the rearview mirror, her eyes wide with surprise and fear, but other than that, she seems unharmed. It wasn't a hard hit, but messing up my already beat-up car wouldn't take much.

"Fuck," I growl under my breath. If ever there was a moment to break my no-swearing around Georgie rule, this is it, but I'm hoping it was quiet enough to sneak by.

"Daaa-deeee!" my cheeky little girl hollers from behind me, her tone scolding.

"Yes, Georgie?"

"You owe me ice cream now."

With a sigh, I respond, "Yes, Georgie."

Yep, clearly, she's fine.

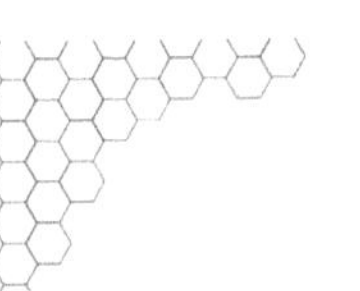

CHAPTER ONE

CHARLIE

I tear down the familiar streets of my hometown in my beat-up old Ford truck; the wind gusting through the open window as my phone blares with yet another call from Mac, the head brewer at Spirit of Hops Brewstillery, where I am, at least for now, the bar manager. I have low confidence in my continued employment if my luck keeps up the way it's been today.

Mac has been texting and leaving messages for longer than I want to admit today, sounding like a broken record.

"Charlie, where are you?"

"Charlie, we're brewing today, and you pulled the short straw. You coming?"

"Dude, Charlie, you fucker, where are you?"

I swear the planets are aligned against me today or some shit. Not only did I oversleep this morning, but I had to run down to The Cities to pick up some supplies my brother Donnie conned me into getting him for his next art installation and then ran into insane traffic on the way back... on a Saturday!

My dumb ass forgot to plug my phone in last night, and my ancient truck can't charge it, so I only saw the messages from Mac about ten minutes ago when I got home before turning around and running out again, cursing up a blue streak.

I fucking hate letting people down like this. I'm not a flakey person, I swear, but I must have some sort of bad juju or curse, or I pissed off the wrong witch at some point in my life because I have the worst luck of anyone on the damn planet. And now I'm frantically weaving through the usually quiet streets of Rapids Bay, trying to get to the brewery, salvage what I can of my shift, and make the rest up to Mac.

As I approach the last stop sign in my neighborhood before I hit Main Street, the notification for yet another message from Mac comes in when I realize I'm going too fast. And just my fucking luck, there is another car sitting at the intersection. I slam on the brakes, tires screeching, but it's too late. The sickening sound of metal meeting metal fills the air as I rear-end the car.

"Fuck a fucking duck," I curse under my breath, quickly tossing my phone onto the passenger seat and ripping the keys from the ignition before shoving open my door. My annoyance surges, and I mutter a string of colorful curses as I climb out of my truck. This is the last thing I need right now.

"Damn it!" I curse under my breath, surveying the minor damage to my truck before turning my attention to the person my shitty luck has inconvenienced. I can't believe I will be even more late to work. I approach the vehicle I hit, a Subaru with out-of-state plates and a bumper sticker that reads, "Peace, Love, and Craft Beer."

The guy in the other car doesn't look thrilled either, and he has every right to be upset. "I'm so sorry, man," I say, trying to sound sincere as I assess the damage to his car. "I'll take care of it. Whatever the car needs, I've got it covered. My brother's the mechanic in town. He's a wizard with cars. We'll handle it," I ramble, my words getting away from me without really registering what I'm saying.

The guy in front of me is surprisingly calm, given the situation. He's average height, around my age, maybe an inch or two shorter than me, with sandy brown, slightly disheveled hair and a scruffy beard. Before I can continue my rambling, I notice the reason for his calm composure–a little girl strapped into a car seat in the back, trying to put on a brave face for her dad. She clutches a raggedy stuffed animal to her chest as her wide eyes stare at me.

"Hey there," I say gently, leaning down to her eye level through the window. "It's okay, sweetheart. We're going to fix everything, I promise." I give her a reassuring smile, and she sniffles, her lower lip quivering, but she gives me a little nod. I turn back to the man, who I assume is her father. He takes a deep breath, clearly trying to get himself under control.

"I'm so sorry," I begin again, my frustration giving way to genuine concern. "Are you okay?"

"Well, accidents happen," he says in a deceptively gentle tone, but I can hear the strain in his voice like he's clenching his jaw. He then glances over his shoulder at the little girl and offers her a reassuring smile.

My heart sinks. "Is she okay?" I ask, genuinely concerned.

The man nods, crouching down next to the car door to comfort her. "We're both a little rattled, but I think we'll be fine."

My gut churns with guilt for causing both of them this level of headache. "I'm really sorry. I'll take care of all the repair costs, and like I said, my brother is a whiz with cars. He'll get you fixed right up."

He looks up at me, still comforting the girl. "That's kind

of you, but let's just exchange insurance, and I can let you get on with your day."

I nod in agreement, knowing that it makes the most sense. My heart still races, and I feel like the biggest idiot. I've never been in an accident before, and now I've not only fucked up my entire day as far as Mac is concerned, but I'm also going to get hell from my brothers for making such a boneheaded move.

I fumble for my wallet to retrieve my insurance information. "I'm really sorry about this. We'll get everything fixed as soon as possible, I promise."

The man nods, his concern softening into a small, understanding smile as he stands, pulling out his wallet. "Don't worry about it. Accidents happen, and no one's hurt, at least. And, well, I'm new in town, so I could use some local help. You mentioned a mechanic?"

Relief washes over me at his response, followed by another wave of embarrassment at my earlier word vomit, remembering what I had said. "Uh, yeah. My brother Donnie works at the garage in town. He'll take care of you, no problem."

His eyes brighten a bit at that, and he smiles again. "Sounds good. Take it you're local then?"

"Born and raised," I reply with a grin. "Charlie Larson, at your service."

I extend my hand toward him, and he hesitates for a moment before shaking it. "Callum," he says by way of introduction. "And this is Georgie," he says, indicating the little girl.

I offer a warm smile to Georgie, who peeks out the window from the back seat. "Hey there, Georgie. Don't worry about a thing. We'll get you guys fixed right up."

"Well, Callum," I begin, my words tumbling out in a rush

again. "I hate to sound pushy, but I'm already running late for work… very late, actually. How about this? Follow me to the brewery in town, and I'll make it up to you. You can enjoy a free beer while we get your car sorted, and I'll get you both some dinner. My treat."

Callum considers it for a moment, his brows furrowing slightly as he glances at his daughter. I can tell he's thinking about the offer, and I'm just praying he says yes. The last thing I need right now is to miss work entirely to deal with insurance claims. He looks back at me, his eyes searching for something. Maybe it's reassurance, or perhaps he's just weighing his options. But there's something about his gaze that catches my attention.

"So, you work at the brewery?" Callum asks, his curiosity clearly piqued.

I nod, giving him a grin. "Yeah, I'm the bar manager there. At least for now, if my ass isn't fired for being so late," I say with a self-deprecating chuckle. "It's a pretty great place, if I do say so myself. It's a Brewstillery if you want to get technical, and we have an awesome mix of drinks on offer at any given time. You'll love it, I promise. And it's always family-friendly," I reassure, tilting my head toward Georgie, not wanting to give him a reason to turn me down.

He glances at his daughter in the backseat, watching our interaction with wide eyes, and then back at me.

"So, what do you say? Follow me, grab some dinner, and we'll sort out the rest after?" I say again, trying to sound as casual as possible, needing him to take me up on my offer but not wanting to come across as too pushy.

I watch as Callum considers my offer for a moment and can see he is about to refuse when the little girl calls out, "Daddy! Hungry! You like beer too, Daddy. Let him feed me!" Her little voice deepens and drags out the last two words in a comically exaggerated way that I can't help but chuckle at. I watch her father's resolve melt before my eyes at her plea.

"Well, clearly, the decision has been made. Whatever the boss says goes," he says with a resigned sigh.

"Great! Just follow me, and we'll get this all sorted out."

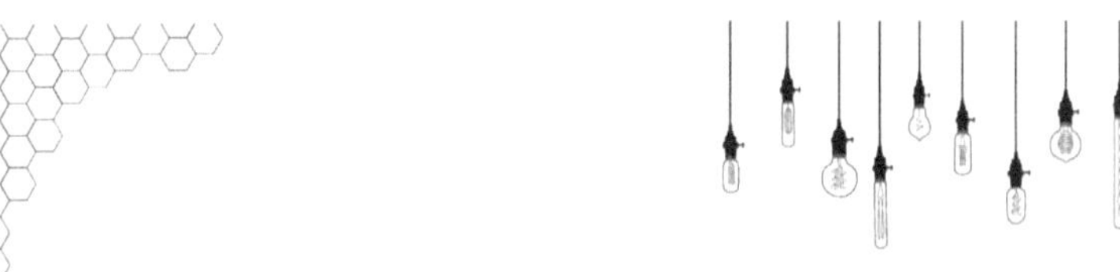

CHAPTER TWO

CHARLIE

I pull into an employee spot in the large parking lot shared between the Brewstillery and Sloan's bar, Valkyrie, and motion for Callum to take the spot beside mine. Waving for him to follow me once he's ready, I take off toward the building and leave him to get his daughter out and settled at his own pace before joining me while I shoot a quick text to Donnie, asking him to swing by to look at the cars after his shift. Before crossing the large patio, I turn and watch them for a moment, tucking my phone back in my pocket. Georgie still looks a little shaken, still clutching her stuffed lion as he helps her out of her seat. Something tugs at me to not leave him to deal with her alone, so I cross back toward his car and watch as Georgie finds her feet and Callum closes the door behind her.

"So we kind of got off on the wrong foot. Start again?" I ask, offering him what I hope is my most charming and disarming grin, attempting to ease any lingering tension. "Hey, I'm Charlie. Nice to meet you, even if it's under these circumstances. I promise I'm a better driver than current evidence suggests," I say with a self-deprecating laugh.

He takes my hand with a warm smile. "I'm Callum, and this is my daughter, Georgiana." He gestures to the little girl clinging to his leg, and I give her a little wave.

"It's Georgie, Daddy. Only Auntie Sarah calls me Georgiana when I get in trouble," she says with a surprising level of sass, and I struggle to hold back my laugh at her spunk. I like her already.

"Hey there, Georgie," I say with a friendly wink. "We're going to get through this together, okay? You hungry?" She nods and offers me a grin as she steps out from behind her dad's legs and already looks less nervous. I grin at her again. "Good. Let's go inside and have some dinner, and then my brother will make sure your dad's car is all fixed up, okay?"

She blinks at me, her big blue eyes bright. "Okay," she says, her voice strong for someone so little.

Callum places a comforting hand on her shoulder and gives her a little squeeze of reassurance. I feel a sense of warmth as I watch how he comforts her, and it's easy to see he's a good dad. That only makes me like the two of them more.

"Let's go inside, you two. Dinner's on me," I say, leading them toward the open garage doors on the other side of the large patio.

To my surprise, Georgie walks right up to me and grabs my hand, flashing me a cheeky smile and saying, "Sounds good. I was promised food and am wasting away!"

There is no way in hell I could have ever expected that response to come out of her little body, and I can't help but throw my head back and laugh.

"Well, we wouldn't want that, now would we, princess?" I say once I have myself under control again. Glancing back over my shoulder as Georgie tugs me toward the doors, I catch Callum rolling his eyes with an affectionate smile as he follows us.

We step into the cozy, dimly lit taproom, where the scent of malt and hops and the chatter of patrons fills the air. I know I should be worried about Mac's wrath, which will undoubtedly come my way once he sees me, but my focus is solely on Callum and Georgie.

I gesture to a vacant table near the bar and pull out a chair on one side for Georgie before sitting down in one across from her as Callum settles between us. The little girl looks around, taking in the new surroundings, and I can't help but smile at her innocence.

As we settle in, I notice Callum studying me curiously. "So, you work here?"

I chuckle at the blush that immediately colors his cheeks when he registers the question we both know he already asked. "Yep, well, at least until the big guy behind the bar over there notices I'm here and feeds me my ass for being so late." It's my turn to color a dark shade of red as my eyes flash to Georgie, my eyes wide in horror as I realize my slip-up.

Fuck, I'm not good around kids. My mouth has less than zero filter, and my topics of conversation are rarely rated below PG13. I flash my horrified gaze at Callum, who doesn't even attempt to hide his laugh.

"It's all good, man. My vocabulary isn't always exactly child-approved either."

"Daddy says *dammit* … a lot. And sometimes other words. But he says I can't say them or else I will get my mouth washed out. Which really just isn't fair if you ask me," Georgie says matter-of-factly. I'm left staring, stunned at her cheeky little self.

Deciding I need to move on before I put my foot further into my mouth, I answer his initial question again. "But yeah, I've been the bar manager here since it opened a few years ago. Been friends with one of the owners since we were kids, so it was a no-brainer to hop on his bandwagon when he wanted to get this place up and running. It's a pretty great little spot we have going here. I was born and raised in Rapids Bay, so it felt natural to want to stay and be part of something to make it better."

Callum offers a small smile. "That's cool. If you hadn't already guessed, we're new in town, so having some local insight is nice."

"Yeah, you had mentioned that... well, and your out-of-state plates are hard to miss," I laugh. "But what brought you here?"

He hesitates momentarily, as if trying to figure out how much he wants to share.

"My mommy moved away with her new boyfriend. So Daddy said we were moving somewhere fresh," Georgie says, the shockingly emotional revelation falling from her little body like it was nothing more than a fact she learned at school.

Callum lets out a quiet groan and closes his eyes at his daughter's words, clearly begging whatever powers that might be listening for strength. "Thank you, Georgie," he says flatly, pressing a quick kiss to the top of her mop of blonde curls before looking back at me with a look that screams, *'Accept that answer and move on.'*

I give him a nod, message received. Clearly, there is more to the story, but there is no way I'm going to press him for it now. "Sometimes a fresh start is all you need, right?"

Callum nods, and his eyes soften as he looks at his daughter. "Yeah, exactly."

Before I can say anything more, Emily, one of the part-time bartenders, walks over to our table and sets one of the flip book drink menus and a laminated dinner menu from the food truck we have here tonight on the table between us.

"Late again, Charlie?" she asks, her arms crossed over her chest and hip sticking out as she eyes me skeptically.

"Aren't I your boss, little girl? That's a lot of shade to throw at someone who signs your paychecks," I taunt back, not taking her attitude seriously. This is what we do. She gives me endless amounts of shit, and I throw it right back, along with a head-pat and snarky comment of my own.

"You wish. Luka signs the checks around here. Not to mention, I'm prettier than you. Mac would keep me in a heartbeat over having to stare at your ugly mug." Well, she's got me there. She's an adorable little slip of a woman in her early twenties who only works here part-time while finishing classes at the college on the other side of the river. She's 5'5 in heels and a hundred pounds soaking wet, but she could easily kick every one of our asses without breaking a sweat. She's my favorite and knows it.

"Yeah, yeah. Didn't your momma ever tell you it's not nice to be so truthful?" I throw her a smirk before turning my attention back to Callum, who's watching our exchange like it's a tennis match, while Georgie is engrossed in staring at the brewing equipment visible on the other side of the partition running down one end of the building. "Well, if you're done busting my balls, Em, I'd like to introduce you to Callum and his little girl, Georgie. They're new in town and had the unfortunate pleasure of getting me as a welcoming committee... by way of my front bumper attempting to crawl up into their trunk. I'm treating them to dinner while we wait for Donnie to get off work and take a look at the damage."

Emily flashes them a bright smile, expertly flipping her long fall of dark brown hair over her shoulder. She's cute and knows it, and while she's completely harmless and means well, she can give me a run for my money when it comes to being a shameless flirt most days.

"Nice to meet you guys, and welcome to town! Sorry about this one," she says, throwing her thumb over her shoulder toward me. "I promise we aren't all like that. But what can I get ya? Beers are on the first two pages, spirits and mixed drinks on the next two. NAs and sodas are on the last page. The other menu is for the food truck tonight. Amazing tacos, and if breakfast burritos are your thing, you do *not* want to miss this one," she explains, slipping back into work mode without missing a beat.

"Charlie!" Mac's bellow breaks through the din of the taproom, an echoing silence falling in its wake. Mac is a teddy bear, but he's 6 '5 and built like a linebacker and usually on the soft-spoken side, so when he's loud, people take notice, and every asshole within hearing distance involuntarily puckers.

My shoulders drop, and I let my head hang on my neck for a moment, bracing for the unholy amount of shit I am about to receive.

"Sounds like time's up," Callum whispers, an unmistakable chuckle in his voice.

I shoot him a glare with no heat behind it before dragging myself out of my seat and turning to face my fate.

CHAPTER THREE

CALLUM

fter Charlie slinks off behind the bar with his proverbial tail between his legs, Georgie and I quickly decide on drinks and what to order from the taco truck. Emily, the bartender on duty, takes our orders with a bright smile and promises to bring something special for Georgie before disappearing out the open garage doors to the food truck parked along the patio to put our order in. I offer to pay and take care of it all, but the little spitfire waves me off and threatens to sic Charlie on us again, claiming it's the least he deserves after all the shit he apparently pulls around here.

While we wait for our drinks and food, Georgie sits patiently across the table from me, playing with her stuffie. The poor thing is hanging on by its last few threads at this point, but damn if I have the heart to take it from her or try to replace the thing. The lion had been a present from my sister when she was just a newborn. Technically, the little guy is a replica of something from one of the animes Sarah loves. Apparently, its name in the show was Kon, but as Georgie got older, it morphed into King Kon. Far be it from me to correct her, so it is King Kon, the ratty lion.

Before long, a giant mountain of a man comes up to our table with friendly, bright eyes and a warm smile peeking out from his dark beard. "Hey man, got a quick rundown of your situation from the dingbat over there. Thought I'd bring your drinks over and say hi, give you a better intro to town than he must have managed," the man laughs as he sets a pint glass in front of me and a soda with a curly straw in front of Georgie.

"Hey, yeah, thanks," I say before Georgie interrupts me.

"Daddy, what's a dingbat?" she asks, blinking innocently up at me. My mistake for attempting to take a drink right away. Rookie move. Her words shock a snort out of me, leaving me coughing and choking on my beer, while the guy standing next to us throws his head back, letting out a booming laugh that I swear rattles the windows in their frames.

"Sorry there, Princess, should have watched my mouth. It's just a name I call Charlie when he does something silly," the man explains, offering her a wink before turning back to me. "Sorry about that. Wasn't thinking. My name's Mac, by the way. Head brewer here at Spirit of Hops. Wanted to welcome you to town without causing bodily harm, but looks like I might have screwed that one up too," he says with another laugh.

With a final cough, I wipe my face with a napkin before responding, giving him a reassuring nod. "No worries, she's heard worse. My fault for drinking too soon." I reach my hand out to shake his massive paw before motioning for him to join us. "Nice to meet you. I'm Callum Bowers, and this is Georgie."

Mac shakes my hand before waving to Georgie and taking the seat Charlie vacated a few minutes ago with a massive grin on his face. "Callum! My new brewer! I wasn't expecting you to be in town for a few more days. Now I'm even more sorry for the crap-tastic welcome you got from Charlie."

"Like I said, no worries. Everyone's okay, and there was only minor damage to the car. It could have been much worse. And I wanted to get here a few days early to get settled in the new place and get Georgie going in the new school before my shifts start," I explain.

"Makes sense. I didn't realize you had a little one when we talked. My bad, I would have offered to help more with the move or something," Mac says. Having only talked to him a couple times on the phone before packing up and moving out here, I don't know him well enough to gauge if he's sincere or not, but I would rather start off by giving people in this new town the benefit of the doubt.

"It's all good. Other than the movers getting delayed by a day, it's been a pretty smooth transition until now. I was headed to get the keys for our apartment when we ran into... or I guess Charlie ran into us," I say with a laugh.

"Daddy said we get to have a camp-out tonight cuz my bed is stuck in the big truck!" Georgie pipes up, looking like the prospect of sleeping on the living room floor tonight is the best thing to ever happen to her. Honestly, it just sounds like a backache to me, but I will never pass up a chance to spend time with my little girl or put that smile on her face.

"Very cool! Sounds like a fun night for you guys!" Mac says, giving Georgie a genuine smile.

Before I can steer the conversation, Emily saunters to the table with a big smile and arms full of containers from the food truck. "Hey guys, saw Mac joining you and figured I'd milk Charlie for a bit more while he trusted me with his credit card, so... eat up! Got a bit of everything," she says with a wink as she spreads the containers out on the table.

Several sets of tacos, two different types of nachos, a massive burrito, and what looks like some kind of riff on elote street corn in a cup.

"Bless you, Em. Serves him right. Want to join us?" Mac asks, grabbing a set of the tacos and settling them in front of him.

"Naw, need to get back to work, since you have Charlie doing all the bitch tasks. Thanks, though!" she laughs before heading back behind the bar.

Mac laughs again, and all three of us tuck into the food. I have to admit; I didn't have high hopes for a food truck in the middle of Minnesota, but damn, I was wrong. Everything is amazing, and the beer is damn good as well. I could get used to things here if this is what it's like.

After a few minutes of quiet, as the three of us settle into the meal, Mac finally starts the conversation back up. "So, Callum," he asks, his eyes gleaming with genuine interest, "what got you into brewing in the first place?"

I lean back in my seat, a smile playing on my lips. "It's a long story, but involves a love for science but lack of dedication to actually go into one of the established careers, a knack for experimentation, and maybe a dash of rebellion against the corporate world."

Mac chuckles, and I notice Charlie coming out from a hallway on the other end of the taproom with rubber gloves and a basket of cleaning supplies. Bitch tasks indeed. He must catch me looking because he flashes me a quick grin before dropping off the cleaning supplies and heading to our table.

It's the first time I have had time to really notice him, and damn. Viking blood must run strong in Minnesota because if he mentioned he was Thor's long-lost brother, I would be inclined to believe him. Okay, that might be a bit of an exaggeration, but still. Close enough. He's easily 6 feet of burly, well-built muscle. Dense, but not overly defined, like someone who built their physique in the gym. No, Charlie is thick, dense, and undeniably strong in a way you can only get from working with your hands most of your life.

"Hey, Callum," he says, his eyes meeting mine, snapping me out of my wholly inappropriate appraisal of the man. "My brother Donnie will be here in about twenty minutes."

"Sounds good, thanks. I appreciate you calling him for me."

"Anything to keep insurance off our backs," he says with a wink before turning his attention to Georgie, who is happily munching away on one of the plates of nachos. "Hey Princess, enjoying those nachos?"

Georgie nods vigorously, her mouth all but overflowing with chips and cheese, and her enthusiasm is infectious. Charlie turns his attention back to Mac and me. I'm momentarily distracted by the easygoing charm in his smile and the twinkle in his shockingly blue eyes.

"Anyway, my brother will sort everything out. Donnie's a wizard with cars," Charlie says, giving me a reassuring pat on the shoulder before heading off to get back to whatever other miserable chore Mac assigned him as penance.

As Charlie walks away, Mac leans in, his eyes narrowing playfully. "You must have something special goin' on. I've never seen that man willingly go back to cleaning anything."

I laugh. "Not sure about all that, but this town certainly seems full of surprises today. Chalk it up to a full moon or something?"

"Or something," Mac laughs.

———

True to Charlie's word, Donnie arrives right on time, his tow truck rumbling into the parking lot not even twenty minutes later. He quickly looks at my car before ambling across the patio and into the taproom through the still open garage doors. Mac waves him down, and the man who looks like he could be Charlie's evil twin approaches our table with a smile. Where Charlie is all blonde hair and blue eyes, Donnie has a mop of unruly dark brown hair tied back at the base of his neck in a small bun and warm brown eyes. None of which distract from his swimmer's build of broad shoulders and trim waist showcased in a plain white tee and coveralls with the arms tied at his waist. If you looked up a stereotypical mechanic in a romance novel, this man's picture would show up.

"Heya, Mac! And this must be the newbie Charlie messaged about. Donnie, one of Charlie's younger and better-looking brothers," he says with a warm smile and offers a hand.

I stand, taking his hand and shaking before his words fully register. "One of?"

Mac laughs and motions for Donnie to take the last open seat at our table as he answers. "There's five of these hooligans running around."

I attempt to hide my surprise by taking another swig of my beer. Five? There's five of them? There is no way they all look like these two, right? That's just not possible. Or fair.

"He says hooligans like he didn't grow up raisin' hell right along with us," Donnie laughs, stealing a chip from the platter in front of Mac. Mac simply rolls his eyes and pushes the plate toward him.

"So, what's the damage?" Mac asks.

"I'll have to take it back to the shop and have a proper look, but it doesn't look like anything too major for now. In the meantime, how about I get you a loaner?" Donnie says between more bites of food.

"Yeah, a loaner would be great, thanks," I say, not even attempting to hide the relief in my voice.

"Good deal. Noticed you've got some boxes in the back, and Charlie mentioned you were new in town. I've got a truck you can use that should fit everything, no problem. And it's an extended cab, so this little one and her throne can fit in the back," Donnie says, throwing Georgie a wink.

I glance at Georgie, who's practically bouncing with excitement. "What do you think, Georgie? Want to ride in a big ol' truck?"

Her eyes light up, "Yeah, Daddy! That sounds like an adventure!"

Oh, to be six again and everything new is an adventure.

With that settled, Georgie and I quickly wrapped up dinner while Donnie and Mac headed back out to grab the truck from Donnie's lot and bring it back for us. Before I can stop them or argue, the two of them are back and have my car emptied and all the boxes carefully stacked and strapped down in the truck's bed. Mac even got Georgie's seat buckled in correctly in the back of the cab.

"Wow, guys, you didn't have to do all that. You're already doing plenty," I say, not used to literal strangers being so willing to help.

"Eh, what's done is done," Mac says with a smile. "But I've gotta get back in there. See ya in a few days, Callum."

"Thanks again, Mac. Catch ya later," I say with a wave.

CHAPTER FOUR

CALLUM

Three days after we arrived in Rapids Bay, and only one since the moving truck with all our things finally showed up, I'm awoken before the sun is even up by a bouncing ball of frenetic energy formerly known as my daughter. What kind of evil cosmic joke is it that the least morning person type parents are always "blessed" with children who think rising before the sun is acceptable? Where is the kid that sleeps until 9 every morning? Hell, I would accept sleeping till 7 most days.

"Daddy, Daddy! Today's the big day!" she exclaims, her eyes sparkling behind the tangled cloud of her curls that has flopped over her forehead.

I groan theatrically, peeking out from under the covers. "Do we really have to do this 'big day' thing every morning?" I tease, ruffling her hair. She swats my hand away with a giggle.

"Yes, Daddy! Because today I start school, and I wanna make a good impresc-, inspec, imper.."

"Impression?" I help her out with a smile.

"Yes! Impression!" She punctuates her statement with an

enthusiastic twirl, her backpack swinging wildly over her PJ dress.

"Alright, alright, little monster," I laugh, swinging my legs out of bed. "Let's make today unforgettable."

We tackled the morning with a mix of routine and the admittedly questionable parenting choice of letting Georgie eat cereal and watch cartoons in the living room while I dozed on the couch for a few extra hours. It's now 8am, and I'm questioning why ponytails are still so hard to get centered correctly. I swear I have been practicing.

The first day of school looms large in Georgie's world. She bounces on the balls of her feet in the center of the living room, her backpack slung over one shoulder, eyes wide with excitement and nervousness. It's a sight to behold—her special first day of school dress perfectly pressed, her hair pulled into a lopsided ponytail, and the very image of a first-grader ready to conquer the world.

"Are you sure about this?" I ask, adjusting the strap of her backpack.

"Positive, Daddy! I'm a big girl now," she insists, standing tall, her chin pushed high in defiance of my image of her as my little baby girl.

It's a sentiment I can't argue with, and as we leave our building and walk to school, she chatters away about what she hopes her teacher will be like and whether there will be recess. My heart swells with pride and a touch of melancholy; she's growing up so fast. It feels like just yesterday she was learning to walk, and now she's taking on first grade in a new school in a new town. My brave little princess.

The school building is tucked into the center of the neighborhood, a long two-story brick building with a gym attached to one end and a large playground on the other. As we approach, Georgie's grip on my hand tightens. She glances up at me with excitement and uncertainty in her eyes. I crouch down to her level, meeting her gaze.

"You're going to have an amazing day, sweetheart. Remember what you are?" I ask, prompting her to remember the little mantra we have shared since she was old enough to talk.

"I'm a mountain. I'm strong, awesome, pretty, and cannot be moved," she says, her forehead crinkling with determination.

"That's right. And mountains don't get scared," I say, pulling her in for a quick hug.

"Right! They never, ever get scared. I'll make friends and learn lots, Daddy. Don't worry," she says, her tone one of reassurance for me, but I know she is truly reminding herself.

"That's the spirit." I press a kiss to her forehead before ushering her inside the bustling school. As we reach her classroom, she pauses, looking at the door. I give her little hand clasped tightly in mine, a slight squeeze of encouragement. She looks up at me with a small smile, and I can't help but marvel at the resilience in her little heart. Georgie has always been my anchor, my reason to keep moving forward. Today is a big day for both of us, and I'm determined to make it as smooth as possible.

Before we can enter the room, her teacher, Ms. Thompson, steps over to us and kneels down to Georgie's height, her warm eyes putting my daughter at ease.

"Hello there! You must be Georgie," Ms. Thomson greets. "We're so happy to have you in our class. Your dad told me you're a smart and creative girl."

Georgie looks up at me, her eyes wide with surprise and delight. I wink at her, silently thanking Ms. Thompson for her kindness.

"Well, go on, sweetheart. Your classmates are waiting," I

encourage, gently guiding her toward the open classroom door.

With a newfound determination, Georgie steps inside, her worries forgotten in the excitement of meeting new friends. Ms. Thompson gives me a reassuring nod, and I stand there for a moment. A lump forms in my throat, but I swallow it down, offering a wave as Georgie disappears into her new world.

Once I know she is settled in her classroom, I make my way back home, my mind filled with thoughts of my first day working at the brewery. As I unlock the apartment door, I can't shake the uncertainty that has settled in my stomach. Starting a new job is always nerve-wracking, but today feels different. It's not just about me anymore; it's about providing for Georgie... and being the only one to do it.

After a quick shower and a change into something that hopefully screams, "I'm a responsible adult," but also, "I don't take myself too seriously," I head out, ready to conquer the challenges Spirit of Hops has to offer. As I lock the apartment's front door behind me, I'm met with an unexpected sight - a sprightly woman, her silver hair pulled into a loose topknot and a warm smile, sorting through her mail on the front steps.

"Morning!" she greets, her eyes twinkling. "You must be the new guy."

"Yeah, that's me," I reply, extending my hand. "Callum."

"Nice to meet you, Callum. I'm Betha. I own the building," she says, shaking my hand with a firm grip.

I can't help but feel grateful for the friendly welcome. It's a stark contrast to the awkward encounters I've had with neighbors in the past.

She eyes me curiously. "And you're the father of that adorable little girl, aren't you?"

I chuckle, unable to hide the pride in my voice. "Guilty as charged. That's Georgie. Today's her first day of school."

Betha's eyes soften. "Ah, the first day. Such a special time. Is she excited?"

"Very much so," I reply, thinking of Georgie's animated chattering this morning. "She was nervous at first, but I think she'll warm up to it. Kids are resilient, right?"

Betha chuckles. "Absolutely. And how about you, starting your new job at the brewery today?"

I nod, shooting her a skeptical look. "Yeah, how did you know?"

She waves off my concern with a smile and a small laugh. "Oh, please, dear. It's a small town, and I've lived here forever. I know things."

"Well, fair enough," I chuckle.

Betha's gaze turns thoughtful. "You know, dear, I never had children of my own, but I have a handful of nieces and nephews and have always loved kids. If you ever need someone to watch Georgie, I'd be happy to help."

I blink in surprise, caught off guard by her kindness. "That's... really sweet of you, Betha. I haven't figured out the whole childcare thing yet."

She smiles warmly. "Consider it a neighborly gesture. I know how challenging it can be for a single parent. And, like I said, I've always loved children. It'd be nice to have some lively company around here."

After a moment of internal debate, I decide to take a leap of faith. "Alright, Betha. We'll give it a shot. I'll bring Georgie down during my break after school so you two can meet."

She claps her hands together with delight. "Perfect! I'm looking forward to it. Now, go on. Have a good first day down there at the Brewery playing with the boys."

I choke on my own spit and attempt to cover it with a cough at her phrasing. There is no way in hell she could know I'm gay. Hell, it's been years since I've even admitted it to myself, much less to another person.

She must mistake the terror I'm sure is etched on my face for nerves because she offers another reassuring smile. "You'll do great, son. Now, off you go. You've got a new job to conquer, and I've got a new friend to prepare for."

I thank her again, genuinely touched by her offer. As I walk away, I can't help but marvel at the unexpected turn of events. Sometimes, the kindness of strangers can be a lifeline, and today, it looks like Georgie and I have found one in Betha.

My FIRST SHIFT at the brewstillery is full of paperwork, meeting staff, and familiarizing myself with the equipment and current offerings on tap. During my break, I hurry back to the apartment to check on Georgie, who should have taken the bus home and gotten dropped off right at the front step after school.

The door to Betha's unit on the first floor, directly below ours, is ajar, and I knock lightly before pushing it open.

"Hey there," I greet, smiling at the sight of Georgie and Betha sitting at the kitchen table, engrossed in coloring.

"Daddy!" Georgie jumps up, her face lighting up with a grin. "This is Betha. She's nice!"

Betha chuckles, setting aside her own coloring book. "Your daughter is a delight, Callum. We've been having a grand time, haven't we, Georgie?"

Georgie nods vigorously. "She even let me have extra cookies!"

I raise an eyebrow at Betha, who shrugs playfully. "Well, we needed the energy for all the coloring, didn't we?"

I laugh, genuinely grateful for the warmth Betha has

brought into Georgie's day. "Thank you, Betha. This means a lot to us. I'll make sure to keep in touch about future arrangements."

Betha pats my hand. "No need to be so formal, dear. We're neighbors and friends now. Just let me know when you need a hand, and I'll be happy to help."

As I leave her apartment to head back to work, a sense of relief washes over me. It's a comfort to know that Georgie is in good hands and a testament to the kindness that can exist in unexpected places. With renewed energy, I head back to the brewery, ready to conquer the rest of the day.

CHAPTER FIVE

CHARLIE

The days since the accident have rolled by thankfully uneventfully, mostly because I haven't had to be back at work since then. After seeing the bill for the car repairs my brother Donnie handed me last night with entirely too much glee, I may have attempted to drown my sorrows a little too effectively. This morning I drag my sorry ass into the brewery for my shift, nursing a wicked headache from the night before. I've got a serious case of the Mondays on a Wednesday.

Mac is already there, tweaking the taps for the day and humming some tune that probably only exists in his head. Seriously, it should be criminal to be that upbeat while in the presence of miserable assholes like myself.

"Morning, sunshine," he greets me with a grin as I trudge toward him.

I squint in his direction. "Do you have to be so cheerful this early?"

Mac chuckles. "Always. It's the secret to my oh-so-happy life. Now, grab a cup of coffee from the back. Kendric already has a pot going. We've got a lot to do today."

I shuffle into the glorified storage room we call a break-room and pour myself a cup, the aroma of the fresh roast doing little to alleviate my misery. I make my way back into the taproom and slump on a stool, nursing the coffee like it's the elixir of life.

Mac joins me, his eyes dancing with mischief. "So, you remember that guy you hit the other day?"

I wince, the memory of the fender bender flooding back. "Yeah, my wallet won't let me forget it anytime soon. What about him?"

Mac grins, "Well, it just so happens he's the new brewer I've been talking to the last month or so. He's got some good ideas and comes highly recommended from the last two places he's been."

I scowl, "You can't be serious. I hit his car, and now I have to work with him?"

Mac's grin widens. "Don't be silly. Not just work with him, Charlie. You're going to work *for* him."

I nearly pull a spit take with my coffee, and Mac's delighted grin morphs into a full-on cackle of delight as I sputter. "What? Work under another dude? That's not in my job description."

"Fuck, man. Drink some more coffee and check the attitude at the door. You know we're all family here, and you already work for Luka, Kendric, and me, so... shut it with that bullshit," Mac snaps, raising a brow at me like he's daring me to argue again.

"Yes, Mom," I grumble into my coffee before taking another deep swig.

Mac laughs. "Life's full of surprises, my friend. Embrace the chaos. Besides, Callum's a good guy. You'll like him. Everyone else around here already does."

I grumble, "If you say so. But if he's a shit boss, I'm blaming you."

Mac smirks. "Look at the bright side. Maybe he'll cut you some slack because you dented his ride?"

I roll my eyes, grumbling under my breath about karma and irony. It's not that I mind working with new people, but working for someone I've already managed to inconvenience by turning their car into modern art is a special kind of torture.

As we finish our pre-shift preparations and I think I've reached my limit of Mac's morning cheer, the man in question walks in, looking all business in a flannel shirt hanging open over a gray tee and worn-out jeans. Callum. Great.

"Morning, guys," he greets us with a nod.

"Hey Callum, you remember Charlie? You guys are gonna be the dream team," Mac says with an evil twinkle in his eyes. Fucker.

I shoot Mac a glare, but Callum extends a hand with a friendly smile. I shake it reluctantly, trying to hide my annoyance. "Nice to meet you again. Officially," he says with a smile.

"Yeah, you too," I mutter.

Oblivious to any tension, Mac dives right into a conversation about his current brewing schedule, and Callum jumps in without missing a beat. Clearly, it's the continuation of a conversation they have been having over the last few days. We spent the day bouncing ideas off each other, and at one point, Mac wandered off to handle some orders, leaving Callum and me alone behind the bar. It's been a slow afternoon since we opened, with only a couple of regulars scattered around at this hour. School hasn't even let out for the day yet, so it's the calm before the storm, so to speak.

I attempt to busy myself with some cleaning and straightening, anything to avoid the awkward conversation hanging between us.

"So, Charlie, you feelin' alright since running into my car

the other day?" Callum asks. My head snaps up in surprise at his bluntness, and I find him looking at me with a playful smirk.

I scratch the back of my head, sheepish, before answering. "Yeah, about that… Sorry again."

He laughs, a genuine sound that makes the tension in the room dissipate. "No worries, man. Cars can be fixed, and no one was hurt. Besides, it's not every day someone crashes into your life, right?"

I blink at him, dumbfounded. Is this guy for real? A look of terror flashes across his face briefly before a carefully schooled mask returns over his features. I find myself intrigued by him. Something tells me he didn't intend to make a joke like that, but the fact that he did only makes me want to know him more.

As our shift wears on, Callum and I navigate the intricacies of working the bar and talking through some of his ideas for things to add to the brewing schedule. Surprisingly, we make a good team—him with his brewing expertise and me with my ability to not mess things up too much. We work side by side, bantering and laughing, and I find myself warming up to Callum. He's not just another employee or boss; he's a guy who loves beer and brewing as much as the rest of us, and that's saying something.

By the end of the shift, as we're cleaning up the mess of spent grains and empty hops bags in the back and Emily cleans the bar top, Kendric, one of the owners and my best friend since childhood, strolls in from the offices upstairs. He nods at Callum and then turns to me.

"So, what do you think of the new guy?" Kendric asks, his hands in his pockets in a non-threatening stance, clearly trying to put Callum at ease.

I scratch my head like I need to think about the answer first. "He's not terrible. Actually seems to know his stuff."

Kendric smirks, "That's high praise coming from an asshole like you. And you didn't scare him off? That's a miracle."

I shrug. "I'll save the scaring off for later. Gotta ease him into it," I say, throwing a wink over my shoulder to Callum.

Kendric raises an eyebrow. "Suuuure," he says, drawing out the word sarcastically. "Just don't go overboard. We need him."

I scoff. "Me? Go overboard? Please. I'm a loveable teddy bear."

Kendric snorts, a sound that can only be described as a mix of amusement and disbelief, and I swear I hear a choking laugh coming from Callum behind me.

"Just don't be too much of an asshole, man. We don't want him running for the hills," Kendric says before offering a final wave to us both and heading across the parking lot toward Sloan's bar, Valkyrie.

As Callum and I are packing up the last of our things and getting ready to leave for the night, I catch his eye and give him a nod. "See you tomorrow, new guy. Get some rest. You're going to need it."

He chuckles, slinging his bag over his shoulder. "Looking forward to it, teddy bear. See you around."

A bark of laughter escapes me as Callum strides confidently out of the taproom and disappears into the dark of the parking lot. Emily slides up next to me and claps me on the back. "You know, maybe crashing into his car wasn't the worst thing that could've happened."

I roll my eyes at her. "Yeah, right. My life was perfectly fine before he showed up. Now I'm all but broke and have yet another boss."

Emily just smirks. "Sure it was."

CHAPTER SIX

CALLUM

I can't believe I've avoided unpacking for an entire week. The boxes have been staring at me, taunting me from the corner of my apartment like judgemental cardboard… judges. Okay, so I'm exhausted from the move and the first week of work and not as quick on my feet as usual. So sue me.

But tonight, I've decided to tackle the mess. Georgie's at the kitchen table, coloring and chattering away, telling her stuffed animals about her first week of school.

Spirit of Hops has been a whirlwind of activity this past week, but it's been satisfying. Learning the ropes, working on a new brew plan with Mac, and getting to know the locals when I have a chance behind the bar. It's a dream job, and I can't help but feel a sense of contentment settling in. With each passing day, I am increasingly confident this move was the right decision.

I'm fighting with thirty layers of packing tape on a box labeled "Kitchen Utensils—Urgent!" and wondering what sort of utensils could be so urgent when my phone buzzes on the counter. It's my sister, no doubt, calling to check my progress. I answer with a cheerful, "Hey, Sarah! Guess what? I can finally see my floors!"

Sarah's voice crackles through the line. "Well, miracles do happen. How's the new job treating you? And how's school going for my favorite little girl?"

"Great, actually. The folks at the brewery are fantastic. Georgie seems to have found her partner in crime with Betha, our downstairs neighbor who hangs out with her after school," I reply, maneuvering another box labeled 'Kitchen Stuff' with my foot.

"Good to hear. Soooooo," she transitions the conversation, dragging out the O in *the* most dramatic way possible, and I wince, knowing what's coming. "Have you met anyone interesting yet? Any cute colleagues catching your eye?"

I roll my eyes, knowing she can't see it, but not caring. "No, you nosey little wench. It's a brewery, not a dating service. And I haven't had time for romance. I'm knee-deep in boxes and brewery equipment."

"Uh-huh, sure. Well, don't forget to live a little. You deserve it, and wasn't that kind of the point of this move, anyway?"

"Something like that," I grumble, knowing she is right, but no way in hell will I ever admit that. "I'll see what I can do, sis."

"See that you do. Oh, speaking of looking for things,... found your lucky socks yet? You know, the ones with the holes?"

I roll my eyes again. "No, and I'm pretty sure you stole them. Have I mentioned how grateful I am for your 'help' with the move?"

"Anytime, big bro."

Before I can respond, there's a knock at the door.

"Look, there's someone at the door, so I gotta run. Love

you," I say, extricating myself from the maze of cardboard in the kitchen.

"Love you too, Cal. Call me later."

Our call ends as I shuffle to the door to answer another knock, half expecting another delivery I forgot about. "Hey there," says a voice I've come to know well over the last week, accompanied by a sheepish grin. Charlie stands in the doorway, holding a massive tin foil pan like it's the holy grail of culinary treasures.

"Special delivery?" he says, almost like it's a question with a sheepish grin.

I raise an eyebrow. "Special delivery, huh?"

"Yeah," he chuckles. "Had a barbeque at the parents' house earlier, but my mom forgot to tell us which one had to bring said barbeque, so all of us showed up with some. Now I'm drowning with leftovers and figured you could use some good eats as a housewarming gift."

"Oh, is that so? And how did you know where I lived?" I ask, barely able to contain the smile trying to break across my face.

"Oh… uh… you know. Small town. Everyone knows everyone?" he answers, looking everywhere but at me and again ending on a question.

"So… brought it over for Betha, but she's not home?" I raise an eyebrow, amused.

"Something like that," Charlie says, finally meeting my gaze with a boyish grin.

Why are the straight ones always so damn cute?

"Well, secondhand leftovers. How could I resist? You sure know how to make a guy feel special," I say with a chuckle.

He grins, slightly sheepish. "Well, let's call it a peace offering for the car fiasco. And, um, your keys are there too. Donnie got everything fixed up for you and wanted me to give you the keys in the morning."

He jostles the massive pan to balance on one forearm before reaching into his pocket and casually tossing my car keys my way. "It's already done? Impressive." My stomach rumbles at the thought of something home-cooked instead of takeout again as I catch my keys.

Georgie pops up behind me, her eyes wide with curiosity as she peers around me into the hall. "Who's here, Daddy?"

I crouch down to her level. "You remember Mr. Charlie from the other day, right?"

"The dingbat who ran into your car?" she asks, perfectly serious.

Charlie snorts above us, almost dropping the pan as he struggles to hold in a laugh, and I have to bite the inside of my cheek to do the same.

"Dingbat?" I ask, doing my best to keep a straight face.

"Well, yeah. That's what Mr. Mac called him, and said it was a name for when he does something silly. I think running into our car was pretty silly."

Out of the mouth of babes.

"Well, can't argue with that logic, I guess," Charlie laughs. "Hey there, Georgie. I brought some food. Want to check it out?"

Her eyes light up, and she nods enthusiastically. "Come in! Daddy! Stop being rude and invite him in!"

Before I can protest, Charlie strides past me and into the apartment, Georgie dragging him by the hand. "Hope you like ribs and pulled pork," he calls over his shoulder.

I follow him, closing the door behind me, and mumble some form of agreement. Charlie deposits the massive pan on the counter in the kitchen, and I can already smell the savory aroma wafting from it. Seriously, nothing beats fresh smoked barbeque. My stomach growls again, louder this time.

"I'll take that as a yes," he says, amused.

As I'm about to thank him, Georgie tugs at Charlie's sleeve, her eyes wide with innocence. Uh-oh. I know that look. He doesn't stand a chance. He looks down at her, but she just takes his hand with one of her sweet smiles and starts dragging him out of the kitchen and into the living room without a word. He shoots me a questioning look over his shoulder, and I just smile and shrug as I'm left standing there, slightly amused and utterly charmed by the chaos that's about to unfold.

I turn to dig through the cupboards for plates just in time to hear Georgie call, "Daddy! Mr. Charlie wants to play a game with us!"

I look over the kitchen island into the open-concept living and dining space beyond and see Charlie standing in the middle of the living room like a deer in headlights. Georgie still clasping one hand as he shoots me a confused and slightly terrified look. I can't help but laugh.

"Is that so?" I tease.

Charlie hesitates, clearly unsure of what the best move is, but stumbles to respond with a placating smile. "Well, I don't know if I can stay that long. I've got a busy schedule, you know?"

Georgie pouts and I'm about to intervene when she looks at me, her eyes wide. "Daddy always says it's rude for guests to refuse something their host offers, right, Daddy?"

I chuckle, caught off guard by Georgie's deviousness. "Well, I meant that for when Betha offers you something to eat for dinner, but I guess this can count, too."

Charlie grins and gives in. "Alright, Princess. What game do you want to play?"

Georgie claps her hands in delight, bouncing a little on her feet. "Candyland!"

Charlie glances at me, and I give him an apologetic shrug. "You're in for a treat. Candyland it is." I almost feel bad for him. My child plays Candyland like a mob boss at a high-stakes poker game. This should be interesting. "Go get started. I'll plate up dinner."

As I plate up the ribs, pulled pork, mashed potatoes, corn on the cob, and cornbread muffins hiding in the massive pan Charlie brought, I can't help but overhear snippets of their game. They have the board set up on the coffee table. Georgie is schooling Charlie on the finer points of Candyland strategy, and Charlie is playing along, laughing at her antics. It's a strange turn of events, but I find myself enjoying it.

Dinner is a lively affair. Charlie and Georgie hit it off like old friends, and I'm pleasantly surprised by how easygoing and fun Charlie is. He helps Georgie with her food, and she beams at him as if he's the coolest person in the world. The evening unfolds in a blur of laughter, undeniably delicious food, and the clattering of plastic game pieces. Charlie turns out to be surprisingly good at Candyland, and Georgie is on cloud nine, having her new friend around.

As we play, Charlie and I chat about work, life around town, and the quirks of the locals and regulars at the bar. Charlie shares some hilarious stories from his time behind the bar, and I find myself hanging onto every word. The ease between us surprises me, and I catch myself stealing glances at him while he's engrossed in a particularly animated story.

As the evening winds down, Georgie yawns, signaling it's time for bed. Charlie glances at his watch, looking apologetic as he stands to leave. "I should get going. Thanks for letting me stick around and have dinner. And, you know, not holding a grudge about the whole car thing."

I wave off his gratitude, following him to the door. Georgie is already halfway asleep on the couch. "No worries, and thanks for tonight. It was… unexpected."

He grins. "No problem. I'll see you at the brewery tomorrow, right?

I nod. "Yeah, bright and early."

"Great. And maybe next time we can play a game that doesn't involve rainbow-colored trails," he suggests, amusement dancing in his ice-blue eyes.

I chuckle. "Deal. See you tomorrow, Charlie."

"Night, Cal," he says with a smile and a wink before turning and heading out the door.

As he leaves, I close the door behind him, feeling a warmth in my chest and a smile tugging at my lips. Maybe Sarah was onto something. Maybe it's time to let a little bit of something more into my life. And if it comes with a side of Candyland and barbeque, who am I to complain?

Wait. What am I thinking? He's straight. Of course, he is. It's always the straight ones. Just my fucking luck. As I clean up the dishes and put away the leftovers, I can't help but berate my stupid fucking heart for its pitter-pattering at the thought of more nights like this… just me, my daughter, and the painfully adorable straight guy with the captivating smile and eyes just begging for me to get lost in.

CHAPTER SEVEN

CHARLIE

$\mathcal{I}$'m elbow-deep in beer taps when two of my brothers, Donnie and Alfie, saunter into the brewery, the familiar jingle of the entrance bell announcing their arrival. Donnie, with his unruly beard, and Alfie, perpetually wearing a beanie no matter the weather, make an odd pair as they sidle up to the bar with mischievous grins plastered across their faces.

"Charlie, my man!" Donnie greets me with an exaggerated and awkward hug from across the bar, nearly knocking a tray of empty glasses from my hands.

"Easy there, D. Glasses are expensive," I chuckle, giving him a brotherly shoulder check.

"What's up, Charlie?" Alfie raises his hand for a high-five, and I oblige. "We need your genius to settle an argument for us."

I glance at the clock above the bar. "Argument? I thought you two were handling Mom's party?"

Alfie nods enthusiastically. "Exactly! We want it to be the bash of the century. Not every year dear ol' Barbie turns 60!"

"Well, it better be better than last year's. That clown incident scarred Aunt Martha for life," I quip.

They both burst into laughter, and the three of us brainstorm ideas for Mom's birthday party. It's a good distraction from the everyday grind of running the brewery. I'm caught between Donnie's grand ideas for the party and Alfie's instance on involving a petting zoo. Donnie swears she's wanted a miniature pony since the 80s. I think Alfie just wants an excuse to play with baby goats.

Once they throw around themes like "Tropical Tiki Extravaganza" and "Medieval Mead Mayhem," I know it's time to put an end to their schemes. Nothing good will come out of either of their brains at this point.

"Moving on..." I say, passing each of them another beer, hoping that's enough to steer the conversation elsewhere.

"So, Charlie," Donnie smirks, taking a sip. Dammit, I don't trust that look. "You've been avoiding the Callum Conundrum. What's the deal, man? You not gonna give the new guys a hard time?"

I chuckle, wiping down the bar absentmindedly. "I'm not the hazer, guys. I'm the peacekeeper. Besides, Callum seems like a decent guy."

Alfie raises an eyebrow. "Not the hazer? Are you forgetting the *months* you spent convincing her it was called 'hops' because it was really dried grasshoppers?"

Donnie snorts a laugh into his beer, clearly remembering what Alfie is talking about before adding, "And decent? Is that all you got? He's been in town, what, two weeks now? Give us the dirt."

"First off, Emily deserved that shit. She spent her whole first week furious that our tequila wasn't tequila cuz it didn't have one of those creepy worm things in it. And we don't even call it tequila, so there's that," I say to Alfie before turning my attention to Donnie. "And second, he's a brewer, not a reality show contestant," I say, glancing toward the entrance. And right on cue, Callum strolls in, and I swear the temperature in the room seems to rise by a few degrees. His brown hair is tousled from the wind outside, and his shirt has a smudge of something bright purple on it. But what stands out the most is the bright pink unicorn backpack, I'm assuming must be Georgie's, slung over one shoulder.

Donnie reaches awkwardly across the bar to slap me like he's trying to get my attention, even though I'm already looking. Brothers, I swear.

"Speak of the devil. Here comes Callum, the brewmaster of our hearts," Donnie coos.

I glance over, and Callum stands there, looking like he's about to face the firing squad.

I can't help but laugh at the not-so-subtle teasing, but I feel a pang of sympathy for Callum. New guy in town, new job, and now he's got the three stooges at the bar, giving him a hard time. I give him a nod and a smile, trying to signal that he's not alone.

Callum shoots me a quick nod as he heads behind the bar to start his shift. Donnie and Alfie exchange mischievous glances, and suddenly, I can sense a storm brewing, and it has nothing to do with the beer taps.

"You know, Charlie," Alfie says, leaning in conspiratorially but making no attempt to lower his voice. "You could make things interesting around here. Spice up the workday drama."

Donnie grins. "Yeah, give Callum a run for his money. It'll be hilarious."

I'm not sure I like where this is going, but they're already plotting before I can voice my concerns. Ideas fly around—switching labels on the beer taps, hiding Callum's tools, replacing the malt with cocoa powder. It's like I'm in the middle of a bad sitcom, and I'm the reluctant protagonist.

I glance at Callum, who's concentrating on setting up for the evening rush. He's unaware, or at least pretending to be unaware, of the storm brewing behind him, both metaphorically and literally, as Alfie accidentally knocks a pint glass off the counter.

But the storm catches up to him when Donnie suggests they fill Callum's shampoo bottle with blue food coloring. I don't know why they're picking on the poor guy, but it's time to put a stop to this nonsense.

"Guys, come on. Callum hasn't even been here a month. Let's give him a break and not send him running back to Denver, yeah?" I protest, trying to maintain some semblance of order in the maelstrom that is my brothers.

Callum, sensing the conversation is about him, turns around. "Give me a break? What's going on?"

Donnie and Alfie exchange glances before bursting into laughter. "Oh, nothing, Callum. Just… plotting the downfall of the new brewer," Donnie says, chuckling. I swear, the man is barely a year younger than me, but acts like he's twelve. And the giant wildling next to him isn't much better.

Callum narrows his eyes at the two. "Downfall? You guys think this is a game?"

I step forward, trying to defuse the situation. "Hey, Callum, it's just some harmless banter. My brothers are just idiots who are entirely too easily entertained."

He sighs, glancing between the three of us. "Harmless, huh?"

Donnie and Alfie exchange a sly look before bursting into laughter. I shoot them a warning glance, but it's too late. The damage is done.

"Come on, man, we're just messing with you," I say, trying again to put things at ease. "These two are a couple of clowns."

"You promised never to bring up clowns again!" Alfie wails. The idiot.

Callum doesn't seem entirely convinced, and the tension in the air thickens. As they continue their good-natured ribbing, I catch Callum shooting me a look. It's a mix of confusion and something else I can't quite place. My gut tightens as I realize I might have inadvertently given him the wrong impression about all this.

Just as we're all caught up in this ridiculous conversation, Callum's bag vibrates under the bar top. We all exchange confused glances, and Callum digs his phone from the front pocket. He reads the message, and a mix of frustration and amusement crosses his face.

"Sorry, guys. Duty calls. Georgie's teacher needs me to bring her a change of clothes. Seems like glitter glue was involved in an unfortunate accident."

We all laugh, imagining the chaos of a glitter glue explosion. Callum glances at the three of us troublemakers and shakes his head. "Leave off the hazing plans while I'm gone, yeah?" he says, his tone sharp, before tugging his bag over his shoulder and storming off, leaving an awkward silence in his wake.

Donnie and Alfie freeze, their eyes wide.

"Well, that went well," Alfie mutters.

I shoot him a glare. "Ya think?" I sigh, running a hand through my hair. "Smooth, guys. Real smooth."

THE NIGHT WEARS ON, and the atmosphere in the brewery becomes increasingly awkward once Callum returns from his run to Georgie's school. Donnie and Alfie try to lighten the mood with their usual antics, but the damage has been done. I catch glimpses of Callum through the shelves of beer kegs throughout the night, and he's clearly still fuming. It doesn't take long for me to realize the mess I've stepped into. My brothers meant well, in their own weird way, but they took it too far. Callum's not just the brewer; he's a single dad trying to make a living to support himself and Georgie. I can't imagine the stress he's under, and now my brothers and I have made his first weeks on the job even harder.

Finally, as the last customer heads out, I decide it's time to fix this mess. I find Callum in the back, heading toward the main storage room.

"Callum, wait up," I call, jogging to catch up with him.

He turns, arms crossed, his expression a mix of frustration and disappointment. "Not now, Charlie."

"Yes, now. At least let me explain," I press, unwilling to let the night go without settling things between us.

"Fine. You want to do this now? What the hell was that earlier, Charlie? I thought you were supposed to be the sane one," he snaps.

"I am, I swear. I had no idea they would go that far," I say, genuinely apologetic.

Callum lets out a heavy sigh, running a hand through his hair. "I don't need this right now. I'm trying to make this work, to make a good impression, and now they think I'm a fucking joke. I'm just trying to make a good life for Georgie here, and it feels like I'm back in high school with the hazing bullshit. I've had my fair share of frat boy shit in the past, and I'm just not up for it. Especially not now. I've got Georgie to think about. I'm not risking my career on a stupid prank. "

"You're not a joke, Callum. You're a damn good brewer, and I'm sorry my brothers made you feel otherwise."

He looks at me for a moment, as if assessing the sincerity of my words. "I just don't want to feel like I have to prove myself to fit in. Been there, done that, don't want the t-shirt. I've got a daughter to set an example for."

I nod my understanding. "I get it. And I'm sorry if it seemed like we were planning something mean-spirited. We're just a bunch of knuckleheads here, and sometimes, we forget that not everyone is in on the joke. Let me make this right. I'll make sure they don't pull anything," I promise. "And if they try anything, I'll be the first to put an end to it… and kick their asses. Advantage of being the older brother," I say with a grin. "You're part of the team, Cal, and we've got your back."

He eyes me for a moment before nodding. "Thanks, Charlie. I appreciate that."

I watch as he walks away, a weight settling in my chest as he rounds the corner into the storeroom. I can't let Callum feel unwelcome or that anyone here is out to get him, especially not with everything he's juggling. I need to put an end to my brother's shit and make sure Callum knows he's already part of the family here without needing to prove himself to anyone.

―――――

THE NEXT DAY, before my shift, I corner Donnie and Alfie in the coffee shop up the street from the brewery where Alfie is working, and Donnie is holding court with the mob of little old ladies. I pull them into the back corner, away from prying eyes and ears, giving them a stern look, arms crossed, ready to lay down the law.

"Alright, you two," I begin, my voice low and serious. "Callum's had enough to deal with since moving here. He doesn't need you two idiots making things harder for him. No pranks. No initiation, no hazing. Got it?"

Donnie and Alfie exchange glances, guilt and a bit of annoyance written all over their faces. "You sound like dad," Alfie mumbles.

"Yeah, well, I kinda feel like him right now, having to police two grown fucking adult men to make sure they don't pull pranks like they're back in high school!" I retort, not letting them off the hook. "Callum's a good guy, and he's got enough on his plate without your juvenile antics. So, from now on, be decent human beings and leave the guy alone."

They nod, sufficiently chastised, and I can only hope they'll take my words to heart. From the very beginning, all of us involved with the Spirit of Hops have wanted it to be a place where everyone feels welcome, especially someone like Callum, who's trying to build a life for himself and his daughter. I can't help if I feel weirdly protective of them. It's probably just a result of the less-than-stellar welcome to town I gave them. But regardless of why, I feel like it's my personal responsibility to make sure they are happy and want to settle in Rapids Bay.

Over the next few days, I make a conscious effort to include Callum in conversations whenever possible, and invite him out for drinks at Valkyrie with the crew after work a couple of times. Slowly, Callum relaxes around us, the tension in his shoulder easing day by day. We find a rhythm, working seamlessly together behind the bar. We chat about everything from beer preferences to Georgie's latest escapades. It turns out she's quite the budding little artist, and Callum proudly shows me a drawing she made he keeps tucked in his wallet.

The more I get to know Callum, the more I realize how genuine and caring he is. He's not just a talented brewer; he's a devoted father doing his best to create a good life for his daughter.

One evening, about a week after the incident, I find Callum alone at the bar after closing time, nursing a beer. I take a seat beside him, a comfortable silence settling between us.

"You know, Charlie," he begins, a hint of a smile playing on his lips. "I wasn't sure about this place at first. But you've made it feel like home. Thanks for having my back."

I raise a non-existent glass in a toast. "Hey, what are friends for?"

Callum chuckles, clinking his real glass against my fake one. "Seriously though, thanks. It means a lot."

We sit in companionable silence, the hum of the empty taproom around us. As I steal a glance at Callum, I can't help but feel a warmth spreading through my chest—a feeling that goes beyond simple friendship. It's something I've been noticing more and more over the last few days, and I've tried not to overthink it. Enjoying the warm fuzzies just being around him seems to give me.

Maybe it's the shared laughter, the easy friendship, or that Callum is an all-around good guy. Whatever it is, I find myself looking forward to the days ahead, eager to see where this unexpected journey with Callum will lead.

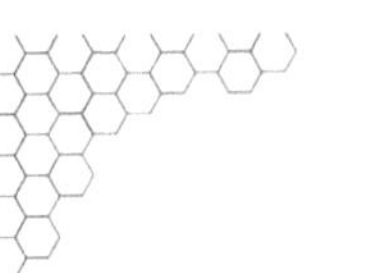

CHAPTER EIGHT

CALLUM

I glance up from the vat of bubbling beer next to me, wiping sweat from my forehead with the back of my wrist. Mac nods approvingly at the amber concoction in the tank. "Another masterpiece in the making," he says with a grin.

I return the smile, genuinely pleased with how smoothly things are going at the Spirit of Hops in the few weeks since I started. The locals seem to love this place, filling it almost every night. Three weeks into my new gig, things have been surprisingly smooth as far as the transition goes—except for my ongoing saga with two of Charlie's brothers. They still dodge me like I'm carrying the plague since the now infamous 'hazing incident.' I guess they're not my biggest fans, but you can't please everyone, right? Apparently, there are two more brothers around here somewhere, but one of them has been on some kind of work trip for months now, and the other owns the tattoo shop in town but seems to spend all his free time over at Valkyrie bar across the parking lot with Sloan, Kendric's better half.

Charlie, on the other hand, has quickly become one of my

closest friends, and a staple in both mine and Georgie's lives. It's funny how things work out. Emily, another one who has become a fast friend at work, claims it's because he has that effortless charm that works on everyone, especially kids. The last time she commented on her theory, I simply nodded along, pretending that's the only reason Charlie's become a fixture in our lives. At first, I chalked my interest up to mere friendship and not knowing anyone else in town. Still, as time has gone on, I can no longer lie to myself about the reality of my situation.

I find Charlie incredibly attractive. Like... unfairly, insanely, pushes all my buttons, attractive. Because, of course, I do. Fate has a twisted sense of humor, making the straight guy at the new job the first one to spark my interest in god knows how long. Figures.

"Hey, Callum," Mac calls as we finish cleaning up. "You heading up to the taproom?"

"Yeah, just need to check on a few things. Betha mentioned she and Georgie might stop by after lunch," I reply, wiping sweat from my forehead. The brewery is alive with activity today, but I'm looking forward to winding down.

As I cross from the brewing area in the back to the main floor of the taproom, I'm surprised to see Georgie already sitting at the bar, her tiny feet dangling from the stool. Betha and another woman I don't recognize are in deep conversation nearby.

"Hey, Daddy!" Georgie exclaims, abandoning her crayons and jumping off her seat to run over and give me a hug.

"Hey, sweetheart! You're early!" I say, ruffling her curls.

"Auntie Betha said we could have lunch at the food truck instead of at home today! And Ms. Josie wanted to see where I draw my pictures!"

I glance at Betha, who offers a quick smile and a nod. "My

niece Josie is a big fan of your daughter's art. She's seen the gallery of it I keep on my fridge," Betha says proudly. "I thought I'd bring her by to meet Georgie today and have lunch with us."

Before I can respond, Charlie strolls in, presumably from upstairs, his sandy blond hair perfectly tousled and ever-present Spirit of Hops branded flannel clinging just right to his broad shoulders. He zeroes in on Georgie, his eyes sparkling with genuine warmth. The man's got a talent for charming everyone in his path, and Georgie... and myself... are no exception.

"Hey there, little artist! What masterpiece are we creating today?" Charlie asks, leaning against the bar with a broad smile for my daughter. His voice is smooth as ever, and Georgie looks up from her drawing with a grin.

"Charlie!!! I'm drawing the brewery with lots of colorful bubbles!"

Charlie chuckles. "That sounds amazing! Mind if I join you?" Without waiting for an answer, he walks around the other side of the bar, pulls up a stool next to Georgie, and soon enough, they're immersed in their own little world.

As the two of them chatter away together, I find myself momentarily caught off guard by a sudden sense of warmth spreading through my chest. I shake off the feeling, attempting to convince myself it's simply pride in being Georgie's dad. Yep, that's totally it. That, and nothing else.

I busy myself wiping down the bar and straightening a few things as Betha and Josie chat to one side, and Charlie and Georgie continue coloring. After a few minutes, Georgie sits up straight in her chair and all but yells, "Wait! I have an idea!" before frantically turning pages in her sketchbook and diving back in.

Charlie laughs at her antics and asks, "Oh yeah? What's the idea?"

Georgie glances between Charlie and me with a mischievous twinkle in her eye. "It's a surprise!"

Charlie chuckles, settling back in his chair. "Fair enough. I can't wait to see it when it's done."

He flashes me a smile before turning his attention to Josie, sitting on his other side, laughing at something Betha must have said. To my surprise, they greet each other like old friends, sharing a familiarity that instantly makes me feel like an outsider. As they exchange pleasantries, I can't shake the twinge of jealousy that nestles in the pit of my stomach.

My reaction is wholly ridiculous and wildly unfair. First of all, I have less than zero claim on the man, so he has every right to chat up and smile his charming smile at whomever he wants. Second, and most importantly, I have no right to get jealous just because I don't like being reminded she and I have one too many things in common... we both like dick, and Charlie doesn't.

I go back to busying myself with random tasks behind the bar, pretending not to be affected by the conversation happening across from me and trying desperately not to think about Charlie's dick. But as the laughter between Charlie and Josie continues, the feeling of being an intruder intensifies.

Georgie, my clever girl, must sense my mood shift and glances up from her coloring. "Daddy, why are you making a funny face?"

I force a smile, reaching over to ruffle her curls. "No funny face here, sweetie. Just thinking about work."

But Georgie's not convinced. "You look like the grumpy cat on Betha's phone."

Charlie, ever the perceptive one, chooses that moment to step in. "Hey, Georgie, your dad's probably just tired from working all morning. Let's cheer him up, yeah?"

He winks at me before turning back to Georgie. "How

about a soda in a grown-up mug? That always makes me feel better."

Georgie's eyes light up like a damn Christmas tree. "Yeah! Yeah, a grown-up mug!"

With a laugh, Charlie slips off his barstool and comes around to my side of the bar, fetching one of the sodas we stock from a small local Minnesotan company. He carefully pours the bright pink drink into a pint glass, presenting it to Georgie as if it were the world's most important creation. Georgie accepts it with glee, sipping from the oversized glass with an air of sophistication only a six-year-old could pull off.

She smacks her lips and gives an exaggerated sigh of satisfaction after her first deep drink, carefully setting the glass back on the bar. "Strawberry, my favorite," she exclaims with a grin.

"See, Daddy?" Charlie grins. "Sometimes you just need a grown-up drink in a grown-up mug."

Damn him. I've literally never been one for roleplay or Daddy kink, but fuck if that word from his lips doesn't have my cock twitching behind my fly.

I force an awkward laugh, taking a step closer to the bar in an attempt to hide any unfortunate bulging he might notice if he happened to look. "Ha, yeah, you're right. Thanks for the advice."

Charlie shoots me another wink before sauntering back around to his seat and resuming his chat with Josie and Betha. I steal a glance at Josie and can't help feeling that same strange mix of emotions. Part of me is thrilled to see Georgie happy, enjoying her time with new people, and expanding her circle of adults she's comfortable around in town. Another part, though, can't shake the unfamiliar sting of jealousy.

I'm not the type to be possessive of someone I'm interested in, or at least I never have been before. I can't say I like this new little personality quirk I'm developing. Jealousy is not a color that looks good on me.

ATTEMPTING TO DISTRACT MYSELF, I chat with Georgie about how her morning with Betha and Josie was, and what she wants to do the rest of the night. I notice Charlie glancing our way out of the corner of my eye. It's a fleeting look, but there's something in his eyes–curiosity, maybe? I can't quite put my finger on it.

As Georgie finishes her soda, Charlie helps her down from the stool, and she runs over to where Mac has set up shop at the table in the corner with his laptop, presumably working on the ordering for our next round of brews. I watch as she pulls out a chair at the table, and he starts in on a conversation with her before she even sits down. Seeing everyone here taking her under their wing so easily warms my heart.

I'm pulled back to the scene at the bar when I hear Josie offering for Charlie to join her and Betha for dinner. My next words are out of my mouth before they even register with my brain.

"Actually, Charlie, Georgie was wondering if you wanted to join us for dinner tonight. I planned to cook something special, and she'd love to have you around."

Um, what was that now? Did I seriously just invite him to dinner? And what the fuck was I supposed to cook? I had planned on ordering pizza, for god's sake. Who am I, and what alien has taken over control of my speech centers?

Charlie's eyes light up at the invitation, and he doesn't hesitate. "Absolutely! Wouldn't miss it. What time should I be there? Can I bring anything?"

We exchange details, and I make up a meal plan entirely

on the fly, spouting some bullshit about how he doesn't need to bring anything since he fed us the last time he came over, so it's my turn. Before I know what happened, Charlie saunters out of the brewery, waving goodbye to Mac and Georgie as he passes their table.

I must look like a deer in headlights as I watch him leave because Josie lets out a little chuckle and casts a knowing smile my way.

"He's a good guy," she says, nodding in the direction Charlie just disappeared. "After dating one of his brothers all through high school, he's like a brother to me. You're lucky to have him as a … friend," she says with a wink.

A relief I really shouldn't feel washes over me at her words. A brother. She sees him as a brother, not a… anything else. I nod, that now familiar warmth spreading through my chest again. "Yeah, I think so too."

The rest of my shift flew by in a whirlwind of chatting with customers, laughter, and the occasional visit from Georgie before she, Betha, and Josie packed up and headed home. As the evening approaches, I find myself surprisingly excited about having Charlie over for dinner.

When my shift ends, I rush out of there and all but sprint through the local grocery store, grabbing what I need for the supposed 'special meal' I've been planning. When Charlie arrives an hour later, he has a six-pack of craft brews from another brewery a few towns over that he thought I might like. We settle into an easy rhythm, cooking together in the kitchen while Georgie regales us with tales of her adventures at the park this afternoon with Betha and Josie.

Dinner is a success, and as we linger over dessert, I can't help but appreciate the simplicity and warmth of the evening. Charlie fits into our little family dynamic seamlessly, and the thought of having him around more often is a comforting one, but one I refuse to let myself get too attached to.

As we say our goodbyes, Charlie promises to swing by the brewery while I'm on shift the next day, and I find myself looking forward to it. As the door closes behind him, Georgie looks up at me, her big blue eyes wide and innocent as she asks, "Daddy, is Charlie your boyfriend?"

I chuckle, mussing her hair. "No, sweetheart. He's just a good friend."

Georgie considers this for a moment before grinning. "Well, he should be your boyfriend. He's really nice, and I like him a lot."

I can't help but laugh at her innocent earnestness. "Sorry, sweetie. You know how Daddy likes boys? Well, Charlie likes girls, so it just wouldn't work." That should be simple enough for a six-year-old to understand, right?

My evil genius of a child gets a familiar mischievous twinkle in her eye before she says, "But Daddy, you said people could like both boys *and* girls. So why can't Charlie like both?"

Out of the mouths of babes.

Well, dammit, she's got me there.

CHAPTER NINE

CHARLIE

*A*nother slow weekday afternoon in the books. Though I can't really complain too much about this one. After opening, it was only about an hour before school was let out. Georgie, Betha, and Josie showed up, claiming their usual tables. The three have become regulars in the afternoons when Callum is working. Though I don't think Callum realized it at first, Josie is the art teacher at Georgie's school, so it's easy for her to bring Georgie home and swing by to pick up Betha before coming here.

Once they settle in for the afternoon, it doesn't take long for Georgie to rope me into an intense game of tic-tac-toe at the bar. My finely-honed strategy has yet to yield victory against her six-year-old genius. As Georgie giggles, making her move on the makeshift tic-tac-toe board I've drawn on a bar napkin, Callum saunters up from the back, wiping his hands on the bar cloth he's taken to always carrying tucked into his back pocket when he's here. My keen senses notice his arrival, but I don't let it distract me from the game at hand.

I have to admit, for someone who never thought about

having kids, I've settled quickly into a routine with Callum and Georgie, much to his apparent consternation. Callum, though a great guy, seems to run hot and cold and has a reserved quality that piques my interest. There are walls around him, and I can't help but see them as a challenge. If there is one thing I excel at, it's knocking down walls. I'm like the Kool-Aid man of emotional barriers. For me, walls like that are like a red flag to a bull; I have this almost pathological need to smash through them. Unfortunately for Callum, my go-to method is annoying people with my ridiculous charm until they crack under the pressure.

Callum approaches the bar as Georgie gleefully declares her victory in our game. I shoot him a grin, fully aware that my relentless charm is about to be unleashed.

"Looks like I've met my match," I say, feigning defeat as Georgie giggles beside me.

Callum raises an eyebrow, clearly attempting to look unamused. "You're playing tic-tac-toe with a six-year-old. Should I be impressed or concerned?"

"Both," I reply with a smirk. "But mostly impressed."

There is just something about this man that makes me want to crack that facade of his and make him smile. I'd say I was flirting if I didn't know better, but that can't be right.

Sensing the impending banter/argument that her dad and I have fallen into so often lately, Georgie grins from ear to ear. Callum, on the other hand, seems to fight a smile. That's good—resistance is futile.

Suddenly, inspiration strikes, and I decide to up the ante. I lean in conspiratorially. "You know, Cal, brewing is a lot like tic-tac-toe."

"If you say it's like a box of chocolates, I'm going to smack you," he deadpans.

"No, nope. Not this time. Brewing is like tic-tac-toe. It's all about strategy and making the right moves."

He sighs, clearly having been expecting another of my infamous puns. I don't disappoint. "And remember, Callum, if the beer doesn't turn out right, it's just a brew-ha-ha waiting to happen!"

Georgie bursts into laughter, and Callum rolls his eyes. "You need a swear jar or something. A 'pun-ishment' jar. Every pun, you toss a dollar in. Maybe that'll teach you some restraint."

Josie, overhearing our exchange, chimes in from her table. "I'm all for that! Count me in on supporting the 'pun-ishment.'"

"You're not even on staff here, Josie," I say, raising an eyebrow at her.

She shrugs. "Doesn't mean I can't appreciate the need for punishment in the face of your terrible puns."

Callum nods in agreement. "See? Even Josie thinks it's a good idea. We can use the money for something useful."

I shoot him a considering look, my mind already whirling with possibilities. "Like what? A fund for the traumatized ears of those who can't appreciate the highest form of humor?"

Callum chuckles despite himself. "No, more like a fund for beer-related emergencies. We seem to have a lot of those around here."

Josie raises her glass, toasting the idea. "To the Pun-ny Jar! May it bring us laughter and fund our beer disasters!"

The three of us clink glasses, sealing the fate of the 'pun-ny jar.' Little does Callum know this is only the beginning of my plan to knock down those walls of his. If puns are the way in, I'm more than willing to become the pun king.

As the evening progresses, the Pun-ny Jar becomes a topic of conversation not only between the three of us, but with the patrons as well. Regulars and newcomers join the cause, pledging their support for the jar. It becomes a running joke, and even Luka, the stoic, broody co-owner, throws in a dollar after one of my particularly cheesy puns.

Callum, however, remains steadfast in his disapproval of my pun-filled antics. Every time I drop a pun, he shoots me a disapproving look, but there's a glint of amusement in his eyes. I'm getting to him, slowly but surely.

With enthusiastic encouragement from Sloan and Lottie, Emily starts keeping track of the pun jar contributions on a little chalkboard behind the bar. It becomes a source of entertainment for the patrons, and everyone eagerly awaits the next pun to see who will be the next victim of the jar.

Things settle in, with the jar becoming a staple at the bar. One evening, a couple of nights later, as the crowd thins out, and the brewery takes on a more relaxed vibe, I decide to crank up the pun game. Callum is busy checking on the tap lines, and Georgie is helping Emily wipe down tables before she and Betha have to head home for the night. This is the perfect moment.

I clear my throat dramatically, gaining the attention of the few patrons still lingering at the bar. "Why did the beer file a police report?"

I pause for effect, relishing the anticipation in the air.

"Because it got mugged!" I declare with a flourish.

The groans and laughter that follow are music to my ears. I glance over at Callum, who shakes his head in mock disappointment. "Charlie, that was terrible."

I shrug, unabashed. "Hey, you can't expect every pun to be a masterpiece. Mediocrity is an art form, too."

Ever the supporter and shit-stirrer, Emily adds a dollar to the punny jar with a smile. "Terrible or not, it's for a good cause."

Callum sighs, looking torn between amusement and frustration. "Isn't Charlie the one who's supposed to put a dollar in for each pun? Isn't that the point of the punishment part of this whole thing?"

Emily just smiles, offering him a shrug. "Whatever works and makes the people happy."

Callum shakes his head with a rueful laugh. "I can't believe I agreed to this nonsense."

"Ah, but you did," I remind him with a sly grin. "And you know what they say about a man of his word."

He rolls his eyes but can't hide a smile. "I also know what they say about a man who won't stop with the puns, and it's not something good."

As the night winds down, long after Georgie and Betha have gone home, I find myself alone with Callum behind the bar. The Punny Jar sits there, overflowing with bills and the remnant of my terrible jokes. I lean against the counter, studying him with a playful glint in my eyes.

"You know, Cal, I've been thinking," I say, my tone deliberately casual.

He raises an eyebrow, clearly wary. "Should I be concerned?"

I chuckle. "Not at all. I was thinking maybe we could use the money for something special. Like a brewery outing. A team-building exercise, if you will."

Callum arches an eyebrow. "A team-building exercise involving puns?"

"Why not? It could be pun-tastic," I suggest, earning an eye roll from him.

Despite his outward resistance, I can tell he's intrigued by the idea. Maybe, just maybe, my relentless charm is starting to chip away at those walls of his.

"You've turned this place into a playground, Charlie," he says, an unmistakable note of teasing in his voice.

I lean toward him, a matching teasing glint in my eyes. "Guilty as charged. But admit it, you're having fun."

He smirks and, if I'm not mistaken, leans a little toward me. "I won't admit anything."

I laugh, the sound echoing through the now nearly empty brewery, that now familiar warmth blooming in my chest. "You're a tough nut to crack, Callum."

"Is that a challenge?" he asks, holding my gaze with a strangely intense look in his hazel eyes. Have I noticed the color of his eyes before now? Even if I haven't, I can't seem to look away now.

The challenge lingers in the air, unspoken but undeniable. It's the kind of challenge I relish—breaking through those walls, dismantling the defenses, and discovering what lies beneath.

As we lock up for the night, I catch Callum's eye and flash him a grin. "Who knows, Cal? Maybe you'll appreciate my puns as much as Georgie does one day."

He smirks, shaking his head. "Don't hold your breath, Charlie."

Challenge accepted, Cal. Challenge accepted.

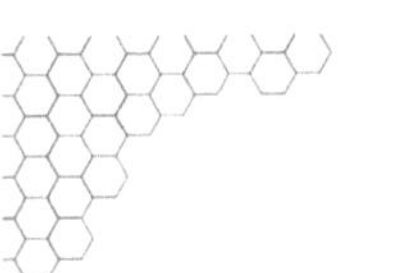

CHAPTER TEN

CALLUM

It's the last Wednesday of the month, and the atmosphere at Spirit of Hops is charged with the energy of the monthly staff meeting. The eclectic group of employees gathers around a large table in the back amidst the tall, gleaming stills, all of us sipping on a concoction born from Mac's latest accidental distillation adventure. The drink, a peculiar spirit that straddles the line between Whiskey and Everclear, elicits approving nods and appreciative smiles from the gathered staff. After a round of voting, it is officially deemed 'Whiskeer.'

Luka briskly runs through the business updates, and Kendric follows with plans for the upcoming Oktoberfest party. As the meeting concludes, the group begins to disperse. Some make their way home, while others, like myself, linger to engage in casual conversation as we all chip in to clean up.

Moments like this really drive it home that I made the right decision to come here. I have been searching for a feeling of family like this for most of my career and was beginning to think I would never find it. Who would have thought the perfect blend of work and family was just waiting for me in a little Minnesota town?

Soon, only Charlie and I remain, the rest of the crew having slipped out in pairs or small groups over the last hour. "We've got this, Luka," Charlie reassures him, apparently volunteering me to hang back and close up with him. Not that I mind.

As Luka leaves, following Lottie, Sloan, and Kendric across the parking lot to have a drink at Valkyrie, Charlie turns to me, a questionable twinkle in his eyes. He sets two fresh shot glasses on one of the tall work tables in the brewing area, pouring each of us a shot of the new Whiskeer. "Time for a game, Cal."

I eye the glasses warily. "What kind of game are we talking about here?"

"Truth or dare," Charlie declares, a mischievous glint in his eyes.

I scoff, taking a cautious sip of the unique but shockingly smooth spirit. "You really think I'd fall for that? Not a chance, man."

Charlie chuckles, the sound warm and inviting. "Come on, it's a classic for a reason. Don't worry, I promise to keep it light."

"Yeah, I'll believe that when I see it," I scoff, throwing back the rest of my shot. "Alright, fine. But no dares. I'm not dumb enough to accept a dare from you."

And so, the game begins. A couple of rounds pass, both of us opting for truth rather than risking a dare in our current states. Questions range from lighthearted to more personal until Charlie throws a curveball, steering the conversation into deeper waters.

"Alright, Cal," he smirks, his eyes dancing with curiosity. "Tell me about your love life. What's your type? Are you… strictly a beer guy, or do you dabble in other spirits?"

Caught off guard by the unexpected turn, I take a moment before responding. I know what he's asking. I've never flat-out said I'm into guys since moving to town. I honestly haven't said anything one way or another. Just the fact he's asking now tells me he's been curious, at the very least. Maybe it's the handful of whiskeer shots in my system, or maybe I'm just tired of feeling like I'm hiding, but I decide now is as good a time as any to answer him. "I've always known I was bi. Well, mostly gay and into men, but you know, once in a blue moon, a bit of latent bisexuality kicks in. It's complicated, I guess. Hence, Georgie," I say with a chuckle.

Charlie nods, taking another sip. "Complicated, huh?"

I shrug, feeling suddenly exposed. "Life usually is."

Charlie's eyes glint with something I can't quite place. "Well, well, Cal. It seems you've been holding back on me."

I roll my eyes, dismissing his teasing with a laugh. "Nothing to hold back. Life with a six-year-old is unpredictable at best. My social life consists of bedtime stories and episodes of 'Paw Patrol.'"

Charlie smirks, inching closer. "So, when did you last go on an actual date?"

I scoff, leaning back. "A date? I can't even remember the last time I had a quiet meal without someone demanding more ketchup."

He chuckles at my glib response. "Interesting. So, you're telling me there's more to the quiet brewer than meets the eye?"

I roll my eyes playfully. "Very funny, Charlie. Now it's your turn. Truth or dare?"

He grins, considering his options. "Truth."

I smirk, feeling a sudden mischievous streak. "Alright, tell me about the last time you were in a serious relationship.

His confident demeanor falters for a moment, and I can

see a flicker of vulnerability in his eyes. "Well," he begins, running a hand through his shaggy hair. "It's been a while. Relationships and the bar scene don't always mix well, ya know?"

I nod in understanding, the conversation taking a surprisingly serious turn. As the whiskeer works its magic, Charlie's questions take on a different tone. "Alright, Cal, truth or dare." His voice has a new, deeper, almost husky quality, and I can't help but watch his lips as they curl around the words.

"Truth," I croak out around a suddenly dry throat.

The atmosphere shifts, the playful banter taking a more serious turn. Charlie must sense an opportunity, a chance to bridge the gap that's lingered between us. He moves closer, eyes locked with mine. He grins, a sly edge to it. "Tell me, what's the wildest thing you've ever done?"

I arch an eyebrow, a smirk playing on my lips. "I guess you could call my brief... very brief... stint as a go-go dancer at a gay club in LA as something wild. That was pre-Georgie, though."

Charlie raises an eyebrow, interest piqued in more ways than one if the sudden darkening of his gaze is anything to go by. "And post-Georgie?"

I chuckle, avoiding his gaze. "Well, my definition of wild has shifted. Now, it's all about successfully sneaking a bag of sour gummy worms into my bedroom without Georgie noticing."

Charlie grins, closing the distance between us. "I like that kind of wild."

Before I can react to his move, he throws me another curveball. "Truth or dare, Cal."

I gulp, a nervous flutter in my stomach. "Not your turn."

"Humor me," he says quietly, pressing in closer still.

"Truth," I say, barely above a whisper. He's close enough

now I can almost feel the heat radiating off him. I'm sure it's just my imagination, but I swear I can feel his warmth drawing me in like a moth to a damn flame.

He studies me for a moment, his gaze intense. "Have you ever been with a guy?"

I blink, surprised by the question. "Yeah, of course. Stint as a go-go boy, remember?" I say with a laugh. "Why?"

He smirks, leaning that much closer. "Just making sure."

The air thickens between us as our eyes lock. There's a subtle shift in the room, a magnetic pull drawing us closer, and it's not just my imagination this time. Before I can comprehend what's happening, Charlie is inches away, and my back is against one of the big stills. My breath catches as he boxes me in.

We stare at each other, the silence pulsating with unspoken words. Charlie's fingers brush against my arm, sending shivers down my spine and all the blood left in my head straight to my cock. The tension builds, the air crackling with anticipation. It's a moment suspended in time.

"Truth or dare," Charlie whispers, his breath ghosting over my lips, sending another wave of awareness down my spine.

I swallow hard, feeling the warmth of his proximity from my head down to my toes. "Truth," I manage, my voice betraying a hint of uncertainty. I know where I want this to go, but the tiny voice in the back of my mind still doesn't know if this is actually something he wants or if it's just the whiskeer talking.

His gaze remains fixed on mine. "What are you really looking for, Cal?"

The question hangs in the air, heavier than any truth revealed between us so far tonight. I hesitate, grappling with the unexpected vulnerability of the moment, feeling too seen and all too aware of the bulge in my jeans that he must be aware of at this point. I open my mouth to respond, but the words escape me as Charlie closes the last distance between us. Our lips meet in a heated, impulsive kiss.

Time seems to stand still as the kiss lingers, the hum of the brewery fading into the background. The tension between us ignites a spark that threatens to engulf everything in its path as he deepens the kiss, swiping his tongue against the seam of my lips, begging for entrance. I give in on a sigh, clutching at the front of his shirt in an effort to stay rooted in the moment as I open for him. His tongue sweeps into my mouth, tangling with mine as I feel a groan rumble through his chest against my palm.

He moves closer, caging me entirely between the warm wall of his chest and the cool still at my back. He has one arm braced against the still at my shoulder as the other comes up, his fingers sliding along my jaw before tangling into the hair at the base of my neck. I moan at the delicious spark the slight tug sends through me, and I lose all control, my hips arching up toward him. That voice in the back of my mind screams to slow down, to be careful, that any moment he will break out of whatever trance he's in and realize what he's doing and run screaming. But instead, he presses closer still, his hips meeting mine and grinding, the unmistakable bulge in his jeans matching and meeting mine in a delicious friction.

All too soon, I break the kiss, gasping for air as I pull back, eyes wide with shock as I gaze up at Charlie.

We stand in silence for a moment, our bodies still pressed together, his hand still tangled in my hair, the unspoken weight of it all hanging between us. Then, with one look at his wide eyes, the spell between us breaks, and the reality of our position crashes over me like a tidal wave. I squeeze my eyes shut, knowing what's coming. The regret, the mistake he's going to chalk this up to, and my mind is too confused, too sporadic right now to play this off. I stammer out excuses, desperately needing an escape.

"I… I have to go," I mutter, slipping out from under his arm and rushing for the door.

The cool night air hits me as I step outside, stealing my breath and starkly contrasting the warmth that lingers from the heated exchange. My mind is a whirlwind of conflicting emotions.

What just happened?

My heart races, and I replay the kiss over and over in my mind. As I hurry down the street away from the brewery, my car forgotten in the parking lot as I walk home, I can't escape the realization that the line between truth and desire has blurred, leaving me on the precipice of something I never say coming—something that might just change everything. I just hope it doesn't change for the worse.

CHAPTER ELEVEN

CHARLIE

Two days have passed since the unexpected and electrifying kiss with Callum, and I still can't shake the mess of emotions that have me tied up in knots. I mean, I've always considered myself straight—never ventured into the gray areas of attraction before, but now, it's like I've stumbled into a maze full of grays with no map or sense of direction.

What's even worse is that it wasn't even me who freaked the hell out. When Callum pulled back, the first thing that came to mind was *huh, I just kissed a dude... and I didn't hate it. Wow. New Avatar level unlocked!* Then the ass took off, leaving me wondering if I had bad breath or worse... bad kisser.

I pause what I'm currently doing to think long and hard about that possibility, then smirk. No, that can't be it. These lips are not just good with a punch line. That line of thinking has me headed south, which, in turn, just has this whole new can of worms squirming around in my head. Those worms lead to Callum, who, let me assure you, is more of a python down under than a worm.

What the hell is with my fucking thoughts today?

It's not that I'm uncomfortable with the fact that I might be attracted to a man—it's the ease with which I'm accepting it that has me questioning my sanity. I've always thought of myself as straight, but there's no denying the magnetic pull I feel toward Callum.

The brewery has become a surreal battleground for me since that night. Every casual encounter with Callum sends my heart racing into a jittery tango, and I find myself stealing glances at him when I should be checking the taps or tallying receipts. His laughter is contagious, and his smile… Let's just say it could melt the ice in the beer cooler. I can't think of a single time in my life where I have noticed another guy's smile, or eye color, much less spent hours of the day obsessing over the best way to describe the exact shade of hazel of his eyes.

Today, I find myself standing in front of my youngest brother Ollie's tattoo shop, a slightly crumpled coffee cup in hand. It's my feeble attempt at a peace offering. The bell above the door jingles as I enter the shop, and Ollie looks up from his sketch pad with a grin.

"Charlie! To what do I owe the pleasure?" he says, setting aside the pad and standing.

"I come bearing gifts," I announce, waving the coffee cup in front of me like a magic wand that will make all my confusion disappear.

Ollie arches a pierced eyebrow at me. "Coffee? You must want something."

I chuckle nervously. "Well, maybe. Can I get a tattoo? Like, right now?"

His eyes light up. "Ah, someone's feeling impulsive today. Sure thing. What are you thinking?"

I scratch my head, stalling for time. I'm about to tell him to just do whatever he wants when an image of a silly purple and pink backpack pops into my mind, bringing a grin to my face I couldn't hold back if I tried. "Unicorn."

Ollie smirks. "Not sure I remember Hulk ever carrying around a unicorn, but I can see what I can do."

"Shut it, asshole. Think Deadpool, then. I wanted to get him added to the sleeve eventually anyway," I tell my brother, referring to the full sleeve we have slowly been working on the last few years featuring some of my favorite comic book characters. So far, I only have one arm from shoulder to elbow done, but I'm slowly working on filling out both arms.

"Fair enough, Deadpool unicorn it is. I can make that work."

As he sets up the equipment, I try to focus on the possibility of getting inked rather than the chaos swirling in my brain. Going under the needle always calms me. The buzz of the machine and its constant lulling sting always bring me a strange sense of peace. Finally, Ollie sketches a rough outline directly on my skin, preferring to freehand when I don't have something specific and intricate in mind that requires a stencil.

"So, spill it, Charlie. What's really going on?" Ollie asks as I take a seat in the chair.

I sigh, surrendering to the inevitable as he sets the needle to my skin. "Okay, fine. Something happened, and I need your advice."

"Advice? From the baby brother? This must be serious," he jokes in his easygoing way.

I roll my eyes. "Funny. Just hear me out, okay?"

He chuckles, leaning back in to start the outline. "Shoot"

I take a deep breath, deciding it's now or never. "You remember Callum, the new brewer?"

Ollie nods, his expression curious but not looking up from his task. "The one with the cute as shit little daughter? Yeah. What about him?"

I glance around, my eyes scanning the vibrant tattoo designs adorning the walls, giving myself another moment to brace. "Okay, well... We, uh, kissed."

Ollie's jaw drops, and for a moment, he's speechless. The buzz of his machine, which is thankfully no longer against my skin, is the only sound in the shop. "Wait, what? You kissed a guy? Since when are you into that?"

"That's the thing—I didn't know I was," I admit, feeling the weight of the revelation settle in my stomach. "I guess I still don't really know."

Ollie recovers quickly, his shock replaced with a grin only a pain-in-the-ass little brother could pull off. "Well, well, big brother, looks like someone's branching out to my side of the road! How was it?"

Leave it to him to make me laugh while struggling with all this. I knew I came here for a reason.

I shrug, attempting nonchalance. "Surprisingly, not terrible. In fact, it was... nice."

He raises a brow at me. "Just nice, huh? Just 'nice' has you tied up enough to come ask me for help?"

I groan at the perceptive little shit before giving up the last of my chill. "It was fucking amazing, okay? Best fucking kiss of my goddamn life, and I can't stop thinking about it, about him, about his fucking taste..."

He raises a hand to cut me off. "Okay, okay. I get it. Spare me the details. I'm still your brother."

I let out a nervous laugh, resting my head against the chair and dragging my free arm down my face. "Sorry," I mumble.

"Feel better?" he asks with only a slight hint of sarcasm in his tone. I simply nod, unable to look at him just yet.

He chuckles. "So, what's the issue?"

I hesitate. "I've never felt this way before. I mean, I've always considered myself straight. It's just... ya know?"

Ollie leans back, the buzz of his machine cutting off as he studies me. "Sexuality is a spectrum, Charlie. It's not always as black and white as people think. You felt a connection with Callum, and that's okay. It doesn't invalidate how you've felt in the past and doesn't have to dictate your entire future. The important thing is not to stress about the labels. Just go with the flow."

I fidget in the chair, his words hitting entirely too close to the mark. "But I've never been attracted to men before. What if this is just a fluke? There's more than just the two of us mixed up in this. He has Georgie to consider, and I just... I can't hurt either of them for a fluke."

Ollie offers me a soft, knowing smile. "But what if it's not? What if this is the universe throwing you a curveball because it knows you're ready for something different? I think the fact you can even consider the wider implications of all of this right now is pretty telling. You care more than you might let yourself realize."

I shake my head. "I don't know, Ollie. It's just... unexpected."

He smirks. "Life usually is. Look, Charlie, I'm not saying you need to slap a label on yourself. I hate labels. Just be open to whatever comes your way. If you and Callum have a connection, explore it. If it doesn't go anywhere, no harm done. You've got to follow your heart, man."

And there it is—the simplest advice, yet the most profound. Follow my heart. As cliche as it sounds, it resonates with me.

As he works, we settle into comfortable silence for the next few hours, the tattoo needle's rhythmic buzz providing a strange comfort.

"So, any thoughts on what you are going to do?" Ollie asks, breaking the silence as he finishes wiping the last of the ink and blood from the tattoo before motioning for me to stand and check it out in the massive floor-to-ceiling mirror on the other end of the shop.

I shrug as I stand, a habit I've developed recently, apparently. "I don't know. I guess I need to figure that out."

He grins. "Well, whatever you decide, just remember to enjoy the ride. And if things don't work out, at least you'll have a cool tattoo to show for it."

We share a laugh, and suddenly, the weight on my shoulders feels a little lighter. Maybe Ollie's right. Maybe it's time to stop over-analyzing and live in the moment.

As I leave the tattoo shop with my new ink, I feel a renewed sense of purpose. I'm going to face this with an open mind and heart. No expectations, no labels—just a willingness to explore whatever might come my way.

THE NEXT DAY at the brewery, I decide to follow Ollie's advice and take things one step at a time. Callum and I have a great working relationship, and I don't want to jeopardize that. As I'm organizing clean mugs behind the bar, I notice Callum approaching, his easy smile lighting up the room.

"Morning, Charlie," he greets, his eyes crinkling at the corners.

"Hey, Cal. How's it going?" I reply, trying to keep things casual.

"Good, good. Georgie's excited about the weekend. She's been asking if we can make more of those pretzel things together."

I chuckle, remembering the impromptu pretzel-making session we had two weekends ago with Betha, Georgie, Callum, and I. "Sure thing. Let me know when you guys are free, and we can make it happen."

Callum leans against the bar, his gaze lingering on me for a moment longer than usual. "About the other day..."

I hold my breath, unsure where this conversation is headed.

"I... I mean... it was..." The sheepish look on his face and fierce blush creeping up his neck to his cheeks is fucking adorable, and I have the strongest urge to lean in and kiss him again, just to put him out of his misery. But I hold myself back. Jumping from "straight shameless flirt bar manager" to "openly making out with another guy behind the bar in broad daylight" isn't one I am quite ready for.

I nod at him and try to put him at ease. "I enjoyed it too, Cal."

His eyes snap up to mine, a look of shocked surprise flashing in the gold-flecked hazel.

"I've been thinking a lot about it, actually... a lot," I say with a grin. "Let's not over-analyze this. We're friends, right? And if there is something more there to explore, we can..." Now, it's my turn to blush and struggle for words.

Callum smiles, the tension in his shoulders dissipating. "Absolutely, we can just... see where it goes. No pressure, no expectations."

CALLUM and I navigate this uncharted territory with surprising ease as the next few days pass. We share lingering glances, inside jokes, and more than a few bills get added to the pun-ny jar. But we don't push anything. It feels right, and I'm grateful for Ollie's wisdom and support.

One evening, after closing, Callum and I find ourselves alone in the brewery again for the first time since the night of the monthly meeting. The quiet hum of the brewing equipment provides a backdrop to our conversation as we sit at the bar, nursing a couple of beers.

"Charlie," Callum begins, his voice soft. "I appreciate you being cool about everything. It means a lot."

I give him a genuine smile. "No problem. We're in this together, whatever 'this' is."

He chuckles, taking a sip of his beer. "You know, I wasn't sure how you'd react. I've got Georgie to think about, and I don't want to complicate things."

I nod, understanding his concerns. "Georgie's important to you, and I respect that. We'll figure it out, one step at a time."

Callum's eyes meet mine, and there's a warmth in his gaze that makes my heart race. "I'm glad you're in our corner."

Between the look in his eyes, his heartfelt words, and the swirl of emotions that have followed me since our last kiss, I can't help myself. I lean in and press my mouth to his. It's a gentle kiss with none of the intensity and heat of the last one, but no less earth-shattering. Neither of us takes it further or attempts to deepen it. Before I have a chance to sink into it, he pulls away slightly, his forehead resting against mine as our breaths mingle.

"Thank you."

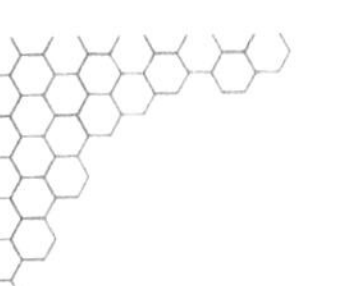

CHAPTER TWELVE

CALLUM

The first weekend of October has rolled around faster than expected. It's another Saturday, and I find myself standing in front of the mirror, adjusting my shirt for the 10th time. Why? Because tonight, Charlie is taking Georgie and me to his parents' place for dinner. Don't get me wrong, I love spending time with the man, but I've gotten quite comfortable with the Simplicity of our evenings at my apartment. This feels like a leap into unknown territory, and I'm not entirely sure if I'm ready for it.

Charlie is picking me up since Georgie is already there with Betha, helping get things ready. As I glance at the clock, I realize he's probably downstairs waiting. I give myself a final mental pep talk about how I should just be myself and enjoy the evening. Then, I take a deep breath and head out the door.

The moment I step onto the front porch of my building, I see Charlie leaning against his car where it's parked at the curb, looking so damn handsome it should be illegal. His eyes light up when he sees me, and he pushes himself off the wall to greet me with a kiss.

"Hey you," he grins, and I can't help but return the smile.

"Hey yourself," I say, trying not to show my nerves.

"Ready for tonight?" he asks, pulling open the car door for me, a move that sends my heart pitter-pattering right out of my chest.

"As ready as I'll ever be," I reply, offering him a brave smile as I slide into the car.

He closes the door behind me, and I can't shake the butterflies in my stomach. It's just dinner, I tell myself, but it feels like so much more.

Charlie keeps the conversation light as we drive, probably sensing my nervous energy. He talks about work, some crazy regulars he had a run-in with the other day, and a few of the ideas he wants to bounce off of Mac and myself next time he has a chance for new offerings. I nod and laugh in all the right places, grateful for his ability to make me feel at ease.

When we arrive at his parents' place, it's not exactly what I expected. There's a lot of hustle and bustle in the kitchen, and the smell of something delicious wafts through the air.

"Hey, we're here!" Charlie calls out as we step inside.

Betha appears, apron-clad and armed with a spatula. "Callum! So good to see you," she exclaims, giving me a quick hug. "Come, help me with the salad. Georgie's already there, probably sneaking spoonfuls of frosting."

"Sure thing," I say, happy to have a distraction.

We enter the kitchen, and my eyes widen at seeing so many viking-sized men squeezed into a little space. Alfie, Donnie, and Ollie are all at the stove, busy elbowing one another out of the way as they argue over something bubbling in a giant pot that looks highly suspicious but smells delicious. Georgie stands on a stool beside them, licking a beater covered in chocolate frosting between shouting and egging them on.

"Hey, kiddo," I greet her, ruffling her hair with a chuckle

at her antics. She grins, her face smeared with chocolate. I kiss her forehead quickly and let the chocolate and eventual crash I know is coming slide. It's a special day, and she deserves to have some fun.

Betha and I work side by side, and it doesn't take long for my nerves to settle. Betha is easy to talk to and shares a few good stories about Charlie and his brothers as kids.

A little while later, a woman who can only be Charlie's mom walks in. She's the spitting image of Charlie and Ollie, minus the beard in Charlie's case and the piercings in Ollie's, and there is an undeniable charm to her.

"Mom, this is Callum, the new brewer," Charlie introduces. "And Callum, this is my mom, Barbie."

"Callum! It's so lovely to finally meet you properly! Charlie has been talking about you nonstop for weeks now," she says with a familiar teasing light in her blue eyes.

I manage a smile, feeling a bit like a fish out of water. "Nice to meet you too, Mrs. Larson, and happy birthday."

"Thank you, dear. And please, call me Barbie," she insists, pulling me into a hug. I can't help but feel a surge of affection for her; the warmth of a mother's hug is undeniable and sorely missed. Charlie shoots me a smirk, and I roll my eyes at him.

"Mom, you're embarrassing him," Charlie laughs.

We settle into dinner a few minutes later, and I'm relieved to find all the midwestern comfort food staples on the menu. The mystery of what the brothers had been fighting over was revealed to be something called "Sweet Soup," a thick, almost gelatinous Norwegian tradition that half the family can't seem to get enough of, and the other half won't touch with a ten-foot pole. I choke down just enough to not be rude, but am pretty sure I'm solidly in the "not with a ten-foot pole" camp.

Once everyone has their plates loaded up and is settled

into eating, Joel, Charlie's dad, raises a toast to his wife, and the room erupts in cheers. After sharing a meal with Charlie and his brother, I now understand why they are all freaking giants. The Viking blood must run strong around here because I don't think I have ever seen so much food disappear in such a short amount of time.

As the dinner starts to wind down and people begin grumbling about wanting dessert, Charlie, in all his charming glory, decides to show off. Grabbing a handful of leftover rolls from the basket on the table, he proceeds to attempt to juggle them. Charlie may be many things, and great at most of them, but apparently, juggling is not one of them. Of the five or six rolls he initially tosses in the air, he only catches one or two again, sending the rest bouncing across the table to land on people's plates, in the platters of leftovers, and one even bounces off Georgie's forehead. The moment of sheer obnoxiousness catches everyone's attention, and Barbie fixes her son with a stern gaze.

"Charles Alexander Larson," she snaps, using his full name like a warning.

Everyone at the table snaps to attention, something instinctual triggering in our lizard brains at hearing someone's full name in the "mom voice."

"Mom, come on, it's just a bit of fun," Charlie protests sheepishly.

Barbie raises an eyebrow. "I didn't raise you to juggle dinner rolls at the table. Have some manners, young man."

"Yeah, Charlie, take them outside onto the patio like a civilized person, damn," Ollie laughs, sending his mom a teasing wink and earning an eye roll from her and an affectionate smack upside the head from his father, if there even is such a thing.

The table devolves into chatter once again, and a few

minutes later, I all but spit out my drink from laughing when I hear Georgie call out over the din of conversation.

"Charles, could you please pass the water pitcher?"

Without missing a beat, Charlie reaches for the pitcher and refills her glass. "Of course, George. Would you like a cookie as well?" he asks with exaggerated politeness, shooting me a wink over his shoulder.

"Thank you, Charles, I would love one," my daughter replies, with all the seriousness of a reigning monarch.

The whole table erupts in laughter, and I can't help but think how lucky I am to have found this quirky, loving group of people. Charlie catches my eye, and for a moment, it's just the two of us, sharing a secret smile that promises so much more than words ever could.

As the evening winds down, Charlie helps me gather our things, and we prepare to leave. Barbie gives me a warm hug, whispering, "You're a good man, Callum. Take care of my boy."

I chuckle, returning the hug and reassuring her I will.

Outside, the air is chilly, but Charlie's hand is warm as he takes mine, our fingers tangling instinctively. The drive back is quieter, the silence filled with the comfortable ease between us and Georgie's soft chatter from the back seat, reliving every moment of the night.

When we arrive at my apartment, Georgie, exhausted from all the excitement, is fast asleep in her seat. Charlie turns to me, his eyes filled with a mix of tenderness and something more. Without saying a word, he leans in, capturing my lips in a soft, lingering kiss.

The warmth of his touch sends shivers down my spine, just like it always does. It's a quiet, tender moment that speaks volumes. When he pulls away, our eyes meet in the dark, and I see the sincerity in his gaze.

"Thank you for tonight, Callum. I know it wasn't the

easiest or most laid-back night, but I'm glad you and Georgie could be a part of my family for a little while."

I can't help but smile. "Thank you for inviting us. It's been a long time since I've been a part of a family, and definitely not one like that. It was a great night. I think Georgie has a new best friend in your mom."

Charlie grins. "Yeah, pretty sure Barbie has already adopted Georgie as the grand-baby none of her heathen sons have given her yet."

We share one more lingering kiss before Charlie climbs out of the car and opens the back door to scoop Georgie up gently, without a word. He carries her up to the apartment, waving Betha as we pass her open apartment door on the way to the stairs, and I follow close behind.

As Charlie and I work together to get Georgie changed and tucked into bed, we exchange sweet smiles and heated glances that speak volumes. This isn't just about us anymore–it's about building something together. A surge of warmth fills my heart as I watch Charlie tuck my daughter into her bed, ensuring she has King Kon with her before pressing a soft kiss to her forehead. I might not have been ready for this step this afternoon, but now that we've taken it, I wouldn't change a thing.

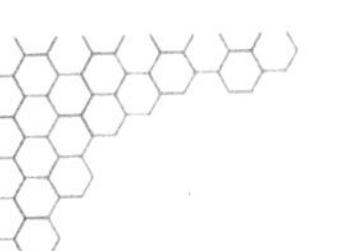

CHAPTER THIRTEEN

CHARLIE

hen Callum and I said we would take things as they came, not force anything, and just go with the flow when it came to whatever was going on between us, I never would have guessed that would turn into him coming home with me to meet my entire family. Or that it would mean sharing little looks and touches whenever we can manage it while working, or sneaking off to steal kisses that are somehow both the hottest and sweetest that I have ever experienced.

I was skeptical at best after my conversation with Ollie when he talked about sexuality and attraction being a spectrum, and how this recent development between Callum and I could just be a new part of myself I hadn't realized before. Honestly, I thought he was full of shit, and I was just having a weird momentary lapse in my regularly scheduled hetero life.

Fuck, was I wrong. I have never felt this level of attraction and connection with someone. Anyone. In the past, with women, things were good, really good sometimes even, but there was always something that just didn't click, or some reason why we never stayed together. It was never something against either of us. Things just always seemed to fizzle out. Admittedly, I went into this thing with Callum, expecting it to follow a similar path. Burn hot and bright for a bit but eventually just run its natural course and fade into the past.

I couldn't have been more wrong. It's just been... easy between us since day one. I hit the dude with my car, for fuck's sake, and he still agreed to have dinner with me! Where I am used to putting in extra effort to make sure I spend time with women I've seen in the past, I can't seem to get enough of spending time with Callum. And it's not just him. I adore every moment I get to spend with Georgie, too. As the oldest, with none of my brothers in anything resembling a grown-up relationship, I haven't had many chances to be around kids since I was one myself. Sure, some of my cousins have rugrats running around, but seeing them on holidays and actually spending time with them regularly are two drastically different things.

Watching Georgie settle into her place in town and seeing how her little mind works has been one of the most entertaining and rewarding experiences of my life. That little girl fascinates me, and I could spend hours just sitting around playing games and talking with her. The fact her dad is gorgeous and has a mouth that seems to somehow act like a homing beacon for mine whenever we are within fifty feet of one another doesn't hurt anything either.

It's been a couple weeks since that first kiss, and where I thought we would have maybe gotten bored or things would have run their course, it's just not the case. We can't get enough of each other. Admittedly, though, for someone who thought he was straight less than a month ago, I am definitely eager to, um, let's say, move things to the next level. We've shared intense make-out sessions, some that involve some great heavy petting and grinding all up on one another. We still haven't taken it any further than that. I know Callum is worried this is just some fluke or experiment for me and is doing his best to take things slowly. Still, goddammit, I might die if I don't do something about this raging case of blue balls soon. Rubbing one out in the shower every morning… and some evenings just isn't cutting it anymore. Something's gotta give.

As the laughter and clinking of glasses surround us at the brewery tonight, I settle comfortably into what is quickly becoming our new normal. Callum and I are in our element, surrounded by the familiar sights and sounds of the taproom and the warm glow of the fairy lights Emily badgered Kendric into stringing through the ceiling to "add ambiance, you uncultured swine." She's truly delightful. But to be fair, she wasn't wrong; they added something special to the place, but hell, if I ever admit that to her.

Georgie sits at a table in the corner, engrossed in a game with Betha and my mom. Betha's got a kind some and the patience of a saint, and has truly been an amazing help with Georgie. What started out as watching her once in a while for a change of pace has quickly become a staple in Callum and Georgie's lives, watching over Georgie any time Cal has to work and handling dinners and bedtime like a champ when he works nights.

I lean against the bar, watching the trio as they play whatever board game Georgie brought along this time. That little girl has a laugh that could brighten the darkest room, and she's got both Betha and my mom in stitches. It's heartwarming to see my mom, who's usually the one doling out advice and running the show, caught up in whatever detailed explanation Georgie is giving in the commanding way only a six-year-old can pull off.

Callum slides up next to me, wiping his hands on a towel and bumping his shoulder affectionately against mine. "Your mom is something else," he says, a smile playing on his lips.

I chuckle. "You have no idea. She hasn't stopped talking about Georgie since her birthday, demanding I bring her over and let her play again."

Callum laughs, a sound that makes my heart skip and stutter and do all sorts of things that can't be healthy for it. "She's great, and she definitely has a fan in Georgie. I like her."

"Careful there, show your hand too soon with that one, and she'll mother you to death before you know what hit you," I say, knowing she's already adopted both Callum and Georgie. I can only hold back the maelstrom that is Barbie Larson for so long.

He shudders dramatically. "I'll take my chances," he says, pressing a quick, affectionate kiss to my temple. It's the little moments like this one that have started popping up more frequently between us that have my heart beating out of my chest and my stomach swooping. I feel like a damn schoolboy with his first crush, and I don't know what to do about it other than just sit back and enjoy the ride.

I glance over at the table, where Betha is now pretending to argue with Georgie about a stack of fake money. My mom grins like a Cheshire cat, clearly having the time of her life. I could get used to days like this.

"So," I say, nudging Callum with my elbow. "When was the last time you took a break? You know, like a real break. Not just hiding in the supply closet pretending to check inventory."

Callum's eyes spark with heated amusement. "Hey, pretty sure you enjoyed that little 'break' the other day."

Damn right, I did. Who knew making out like horny high schoolers while on the clock and hiding from your coworkers could be so fucking hot? Though, admittedly, there was a bit of a learning curve I hadn't expected that came back to bite me in the ass during that particular make-out session. Who knew sucking face with another guy like his mouth was your lifeline when you both have rather glorious beards could result in said glorious beards getting a little tangled and stuck together? Yeah. Not our most graceful moment.

The memory of that encounter has my face heating and my cock taking notice, but I try to cover it with a cough while I reach down to adjust my fly as surreptitiously as possible. "Ass," I say through another cough. "You know damn well I did. But that's not what I meant, smartass."

Callum throws his head back and lets out a deep, full-bodied laugh at my predicament, the sound carrying through the taproom and drawing a few patrons' attention. Dick.

When he gets control of himself again, he dramatically wipes away fake tears before continuing the conversation with a wink. "So, are you suggesting I'm a workaholic?"

I give him an exaggerated look. "Me? Never."

He chuckles again. "Okay, okay. Maybe I could use a break."

"That's the spirit!" I declare. "How about we go on a date this weekend? Like a *real* date. No brewery, no Georgie. Just you and me."

Callum raises an eyebrow at me with a sly grin. "Why, Charlie Larson, are you asking me out?"

I feign offense. "Of course not! I'm just suggesting that a certain brewer needs to loosen up and have a little fun."

He smirks. "Fun, huh?"

I nod solemnly. "It's a revolutionary concept, I know. But I think we can pull it off."

As we banter back and forth, our exchange getting increasingly suggestive and downright dirty, my mom catches wind of our conversation when she comes up to grab a refill. She leans against the bar across from us, giving us a wink. "Do I hear date talk? About time! I'll watch Georgie for you. You kids go and enjoy yourself."

I glance at Callum, who looks a bit unsure. The man is an amazing father, but it's not hard to see he's a little overprotective of Georgie. She's his world, and other than a sister back in Denver he talks to every once in a while, Georgie's all he's got. I can't blame him for being anxious to leave her with someone new.

Barbie, ever the opportunist, seizes the moment. "It'll be a girl's night!" she says, clapping her hands excitedly before calling over her shoulder across the entire taproom. "Betha! Girl's night! You're invited too!"

Betha looks up from the game, and Georgie, bouncing in her seat, giggles and claps along, too. "Girl's night? Why not? Sounds fun!"

Callum looks at me, and I can see the hesitation in his eyes. Sensing her dad's reluctance, Georgie hops out of her seat at the table and sprints over to the bar, crawling up on one of the barstools with Barbie's assistance. Sitting on her knees on the tall stool, she braces both palms on the bar across from her dad and levels him with the most deadpan expression a six-year-old can muster.

"Dad. Don't be a buzzard killer."

I snort a laugh, choking on my own spit at her absolutely perfect delivery. The cheek of this kid is amazing.

"Buzzkill," Callum corrects, trying to hide his smile. Then continues, "And how do you even know that word, little lady?" Callum asks, dumbfounded.

"Donnie," she replies with a shrug, like it's the most

obvious answer in the world. Which, knowing my brother, it kind of is.

"Yeah, that tracks," my mom says with a laugh.

"Seriously, Dad. Will you go now, please? I need a girl's night, too."

And just like that, Callum's resistance crumbles. He chuckles, reaching across the bar to tousle Georgie's curls. "Okay, okay. You win. You can have a girl's night with Barbie and Betha this weekend."

"You hear that, Nana Barbie?! We can have a girl's night!" Georgie all but squeals, standing up on her stool and launching herself at my mom, who catches her and gives her a tight squeeze before lowering her to the ground with a giant smile on her face.

"You bet I did, Gigi! It'll be a blast!"

Before either Callum or I can say anything, my mom takes Georgie by the hand and leads her back to the table to resume their game with Betha.

"Um, what just happened? And when did 'Nana Barbie' become a thing?" Callum asks, shooting me a dazed and confused expression. Seriously, this man is adorable. And the fact that I can stand here and call another man adorable and absolutely mean it really should tell you everything you need to know about where my feelings are at right now.

"That, my dear Cal, was Barbie Larson at her finest," I answer with a grin.

With that settled, Callum and I exchange a look that starts tentatively but quickly gains momentum until we both have stupid, shit-eating grins. We're going on a date. A real, grown-up date. The prospect is exciting and nerve-wracking all at once.

The evening continues, the atmosphere in the taproom buzzing with energy. Callum and I steal glances and smiles whenever we can, both of us already planning the weekend.

A date. It sounds so simple, but for us, it's a step into uncharted territory, a chance to explore this thing between us without anyone or anything else getting in the way.

God, I hope that includes getting our pants, or all our clothes, really, out of the way, too.

CHAPTER FOURTEEN

CALLUM

"**Y**ou don't have neighbors anymore, right?" Charlie asks as he follows me down the short hallway to my apartment door, his hand firmly planted on my lower back, all but pushing me along.

"Well, considering Betha is over at your mom's with her and Georgie tonight, it's safe to say it's just you and I in the building tonight. The beauty of a duplex," I say with a chuckle. I wasn't sure what to expect from this date night, but Charlie has been dropping hints he's ready for more for a while now, not to mention how the man couldn't keep his hands to himself while we were at dinner earlier tonight. I know I have been hesitant to push for more; the guy thought he was straight a month ago, for god's sake! But when he flashes those fucking baby blues my way, I know I will give that man anything.

He chuckles beside me as we reach my door, and I fumble with the lock. "Good," he says, kissing the back of my neck.

I hum at the feel of his warmth against me and his soft lips teasing below my ear. "Why's that?" I ask, distracted and forgetting all about the task at hand.

"Just making sure you aren't going to get us arrested tonight," he teases, and I can feel his grin against my skin.

"Okay, okay, horndog. Don't get ahead of yourself," I say, shrugging him off of me and returning to my task of unlocking the apartment door. When I finally get it open and step inside, I turn back to him with a smirk. "I believe I was promised a movie that doesn't involve cartoon princesses or talking animals."

Charlie grumbles as he steps inside, but I know he's on board from the teasing glint in his eyes. Apparently, the desire to do anything for the other person is a quality we share in this relationship.

We quickly settle in, kicking off shoes and tossing jackets over the back of kitchen chairs before tumbling onto the couch in a heap, both reaching for the remote on the coffee table.

"Nope," he says, snatching the remote and tucking it behind his back as I make another grab for it. "You chose last night. It's my turn."

"Watching Labyrinth with my six-year-old doesn't count as choosing!" I argue, ducking to the side to reach for the remote again.

"Pretty sure getting to stare at David Bowie's junk in those pants all night counts," he says, the teasing glint in his eyes making my stomach swoop. I can see where this is going, and dammit, if I have any will to resist him left.

"Totally doesn't count. And I wasn't the one remarking on said package all damn night," I shoot back, no heat behind the words.

"That's beside the point. Even Georgie agreed with me his pants, and I quote, 'look weird,'" he says with a grin, passing the remote from one hand to the other and holding it out to the side, out of my reach.

I jump for the remote, trying to grab it from him, but he

leans back, keeping it out of my reach and causing me to land in an awkward heap sprawled half across his chest and lap. "Oh my god, you are such a child," I laugh.

Without acknowledging my awkward position or my words, Charlie turns to look at the TV, his arm still stretched out as far away from me as it can as he flicks on the screen and starts scrolling through Netflix without a care.

"You really don't have to fight me on this, you know," I say, attempting to sound annoyed but failing miserably as I press back up to sitting, my hand on his thigh for leverage.

"But it's more fun this way, babe," he says, shooting me a wink over his shoulder. That one word, that endearment, has my breath catching and my hand flexing involuntarily against his thigh. It's the first time he's called me something like that, and it does something to me. My heart twists, and my stomach flips, and I can't hold back a smile.

Not wanting to let my suddenly sappy mood ruin the playful atmosphere, I tuck those feelings into the back of my mind for later, and continue with this ridiculous fake battle for the remote. "Let me see it," I say, reaching out.

"Not gonna happen," he says, holding it just a little farther away.

We grapple with each other. He's bigger than me and stronger, but not by much, and what I lack in height or reach, I make up for by being scrappier and more determined. We roll off the couch, landing on the floor with a loud thud as I finally wrestle the little device away from him. My head bounces off the rug when we land, not hard enough to hurt or do any real damage but enough to stun me for a second. Just long enough for my grip on the remote to loosen. Charlie pulls it free, holding it over our heads, out of my reach, his other arm pressing my chest into the floor.

"Ha!" he crows.

My eyes narrow. "I will not lose." I lunge upward,

knocking him off balance and down onto the rug. He's stunned, the breath rushing out of him, and I take the opportunity to grab his wrist and try to force the remote out of his grip.

"Fuck!" he swears, struggling to maintain his hold. "Give it up already!"

"Never!" I declare dramatically.

His knee comes up between us, barely missing making contact with my crotch. I grunt instinctively, momentarily distracted, but it gives him the chance he needs. He bucks and twists his body, rolling me off him. I let go of his arm and land heavily on my back again. He's quick, springing up to standing, his feet on either side of my hips.

"Ha!" he crows again, waving the remote above his head. "I win."

I look up at him, my eyes raking along the tall expanse of his body as he looms over me, appreciating every inch. When my gaze finally meets his, there's no mistaking the heat in mine. "Are you sure?"

He blinks. "Uh, yeah. I have the remote."

"Then drop it," I say, my voice a husky purr as I slowly trail my hands over the tops of his feet, up his ankles, and begin making my way up his calves.

I see him visibly swallow as he watches me, his gaze heating but still a little uncertain. One part of him clearly isn't uncertain, though, judging by the rapidly growing bulge in the front of his jeans.

"Why?" he croaks, his eyes never leaving mine.

Slowly, I contract my stomach muscles and crunch up, my hands trailing from his calves, over the back of his knees, and resting on the outside of his thighs as I come to sit. "I have a better idea for something we can do," I say with an evil smirk.

"Oh," he says.

The remote drops from his fingers, bouncing on the rug.

I smirk, leaning forward, my fingers tensing against his thighs as I brush my nose over the bulge in his jeans that's now perfectly at eye level.

He groans, letting his head fall back on his neck, his hands clenched into fists and unclenching at his sides.

"This is better than Netflix, isn't it?" I murmur against him, intentionally exhaling against his jeans as a ghost my lips over him, letting him feel the heat of my breath through the fabric.

"Fuck," he gasps.

"You on board?" I ask, my hands skimming up to cup his ass and lightly squeeze.

"Yes," he moans, his head falling forward, his chin dropping to his chest as he looks down at me, meeting my gaze once again.

With a grin, I move my hands from his ass and quickly tug open his belt and pop open the button of his jeans before leaning up and snagging the zipper with my teeth. Without breaking eye contact, I slowly tug his zipper down, watching as his eyes darken and his pupils blow wide with desire with each click of the little metal teeth as they come undone. His fists are clenching and unclenching in a rapid rhythm and his breaths are coming in quick pants by the time I'm done.

"Fuck, Cal," he groans, sounding almost pained.

I smirk up at him while my hands move to tug at the waistband of his jeans and tight black boxer briefs beneath. "Want me to stop?" I tease.

"Don't you fucking dare," he all but growls, some of his control finally snapping as he brushes my hands away and shoves down his pants and boxers in one fluid motion, leaving them bunched at his knees. His perfect cock slapped against his stomach with the move, leaving a small wet spot on his gray tee from the precum already pooling at the tip. It stood proudly from a nest of neatly trimmed curls at his groin, deliciously long and perfectly thick. My mouth watered at just the look of him, desperate for a taste.

"Wouldn't dream of it," I breathe, leaning in close and letting my warm breath tickle the sensitive skin of his balls, making him shudder. My hands ghost over his thighs, the coarse hairs there raising with goosebumps as I skim my palms over them and back around to grip his ass. Tilting my face up just slightly, I run my tongue up the underside of his erection before swirling my tongue around the head, already swollen and an angry reddish purple with desire.

"Fuck Cal..." Charlie pants, but his words die away when the tip of my tongue dips into his slit, lapping up the sweet little bead of precum that wells up to meet me there. I hum in satisfaction, sucking the head between my parted lips.

"Holy shit," he chokes out, his hands giving up the fight of restraint and tangling into my hair. I chuckle as I watch Charlie's eyes roll back in his head and feel the muscles under my hands tremble, his legs threatening to give out. "You're going to make me cum so fast, baby," he groans from above me.

I pull back, the tip of his cock leaving my lips with an obscene pop. I grin up at him. "Nah, just getting started."

Before he can respond, my tongue circles the tip of his cock again, once, twice, before I lean in again to press closer, swallowing his entire length, hollowing my cheeks, and sucking hard.

"Fuck!" he gasps, his muscles spasming under my palms and his fists tugging sharply at their hold in my hair. I hold him there, his cock pressing into my throat as my nose nestles against the soft curls at his groin, reveling in the feel of him filling me like this, dreaming of feeling this full in other ways soon as well. After a moment, I feel his muscles relax just that little bit, enough to tell me he isn't right on edge at least, and I take that as my cue to move. Releasing the suction just slightly, I pull back on his length, dragging my lips and swirling my tongue as I go, letting my eyes drift close as I find a rhythm.

"Damn, you look fucking perfect with your lips stretched around my cock," Charlie groans, and I hum around him in contentment. I can't deny that a little part of me worried he would freak out when we really got down to it. Still, judging by the sounds he's making and the steel pipe of a dick currently prodding at the back of my throat, I think we are in the clear on that front.

Using my hold on his ass, I move over his length, encouraging him to move with me and fuck my face if he wants. I take him deep, sucking, slurping, and moaning as he takes my hint and uses his hold on my hair to take some control of my movements. It doesn't take long before I feel the telltale swelling of the head of his cock and ease off, knowing he's on the edge but unwilling to let him fall over just yet.

He groans in protest but loosens his grip on my hair enough to let me move.

"Fucking hell, slow down, I'm right fucking there," he pants.

"I know, but I like sucking you," I tease, pulling my mouth away and grinning up at him.

"God, you fucking tease," he growls before leaning down, his lips meeting mine in a fierce kiss, his tongue forcing its way into my mouth and making me moan. He kisses me breathless, devouring me and swallowing each moan and groan he drags from me.

Finally, he breaks the kiss, using his hold on my hair to tug my head back further, exposing my neck to him. I watch his eyes follow the movement of my Adam's apple as I swallow before he meets my eyes again, staring down at me with more raw need and hunger than I have ever seen from another person.

"You know," he says, his voice like gravel. "This would be easier if we were both naked."

"Is that so?" I ask, raising a brow in challenge.

"Damn right," he says, straightening to stand and taking an awkward step back, his jeans around his knees hindering his movements. "Up," he growls at me.

"Demanding, aren't we?" I tease, scooting back a bit to pull my legs out from between his feet.

"Yes. And I don't hear a complaint."

"Not a one," I say, grinning up at him as I go to stand.

"Good, now come 'ere," he says, reaching for me again.

"You always like this?" I ask with a laugh as I let him tug me against him, our chests pressing together as his arms come around me.

"Sometimes," he admits with a grin.

"I like it."

"So do I," he murmurs, nuzzling against my jaw. His hands wander from my back, over my ass, pausing to knead the muscles there for a moment before coming around to tug at my belt.

"Off," he demands, his lips finding the soft spot behind my ear as he gets my belt buckle undone.

"What, in some kind of hurry?" I ask, my hands doing some wandering of their own, finding their way under the hem of his tee to tease at the firm muscles of his back.

With a growl he takes a step back, shooting me a glare. "Pants. Off. Or I won't touch your cock. I'll make you watch."

"You wouldn't dare," I challenge.

"Don't test me, baby."

Christ. I can't hold back the full body shudder at his words. Baby. Fuck. The words make my balls ache. Something about that one word makes me lose any and all composure. I lunge forward, kissing him, our lips and tongues colliding and clashing. His hips buck against me, his hands fumble with the fastening of my jeans as I tug at the hem of his shirt, attempting to ruck it up and off him without breaking the kiss.

Before my brain registers the move, Charlie gives me a shove and sends me tumbling back against the couch, his body following mine down as he tugs my jeans down and off, and then he's laying over me, our tongues tangling again as our hips grind together, our cocks rubbing in a delicious friction.

"Oh, fuck, fuck," I gasp, arching up under him, the feeling of his erection against mine sending me cross-eyed with the pleasure of it. "Fuck me," I plead. I hadn't meant to say it, to beg for it. Hell, I hadn't gone into the date tonight expecting it to happen regardless of configuration, but now, with his solid weight against me and his heated cock driving against mine, I can't imagine tonight going any other way. I need him. Need his cock. It's been entirely too long since I've had anything even remotely that satisfying anywhere near me, and there is no way I am letting another minute go by without claiming every damn inch of what I want.

CHAPTER FIFTEEN

CHARLIE

Nothing. Nothing has ever felt so good, or so right, as having Callum Bowers beneath me. I know I had been talking a big game leading up to tonight, thinking I had everything figured out and knew what I was getting into. But I had no clue. Not a single damn clue what the reality of what being with a man like Callum could be like. It wasn't just the obvious "he's a dude, and there's two dicks involved now" thing that left me reeling... it was the connection, the hunger, the desperate and insatiable need to touch and be touched in a way I have never experienced with another partner before. It was fucking breathtaking.

And holy fuck, can the man suck cock. If *that's* what it's like to have another dude suck my dick, sign me the fuck up. No. That's wrong. I don't want just any dude. I want him. I want Callum. I need him.

Hearing him beg me to fuck him wasn't something I had prepared for, for some reason. As he arches beneath me, his head thrown back, eyes closed in pleasure as he begs, I pause, taking in the sight of him. He's gorgeous, spread out in wanton abandon like this, and it takes my breath away.

Something about the image of his Adam's apple bobbing as he struggles to swallow around a groan when I give my hips another little swivel finally breaks whatever reverie had a hold on me, and I grin. Slotting my hips more firmly against his in our awkward position, half on and half off the couch, I press up and lean back as I tug his shirt off before leaning in and biting and licking the new expanse of skin exposed to me. My teeth find his nipple, and I give it a little tug, and he cries out.

"Dammit," he growls, his hands pushing me away.

I fall back, sliding off him to land on my knees and sit back on my heels, wondering what I did wrong to make him push me away. "What?" I ask, my brow furrowing. Was it the biting? Is that not a thing with guys? Maybe?

"Lube. Condoms," he hisses, awkwardly struggling to stand before darting off down the hall, presumably to his bedroom to grab supplies.

"Shit," I laugh, dragging a hand down my face as I collect myself and try to slow my heart rate and beat back the moment of panic. I hadn't done anything wrong. We were good. More than good if his little Flash impression was anything to go by. Deciding to take advantage of his momentary absence, I quickly kick off the last of my clothes before sitting and making myself comfortable in the middle of his couch. It takes me two point five seconds before I get impatient with waiting, my cock feeling lonely and cold without his delectable body pressed against me. Slowly, I stroke myself, images of what we've already done and what I can't wait to do to him rushing through my head almost faster than I can follow. Gripping myself tightly at the base to stave off the impending orgasm I feel building at the base of my spine, I lean my head back against the back of the couch and let out a groan.

"You started without me," Callum's voice calls from some-where nearby, an unmistakable pout in his tone.

"You took too long," I say, my hand continuing its slow movements along my cock as I lazily roll my head to the side, not lifting it from the couch and opening my eyes just enough to see him.

He grins back at me from the entry to the hallway, finally naked and no doubt enjoying the debauched picture I must be painting at the moment. "Guess I'll have to give you some-thing else to do," he teases.

"Like what?" I ask, taking the bait.

"How about this?" he asks, stepping forward and setting down the condoms and lube on the coffee table before his hand closes around my length, just above my own grip.

I let out a moan, dropping my hand away, giving him free rein.

"Or maybe this," he murmurs, leaning down to run his tongue around the crown of my cock, lapping at the steady trickle of precum his ministrations are eliciting.

A sound escapes me, something between a groan and a whimper at the feel of his tongue against me again. I swear I've died and gone to the heaven that is this man's mouth.

"Or maybe this," he says, turning around and grabbing the supplies again, tossing a condom onto the couch next to me before popping the cap on the lube. Without another word, he crawls up, his knees bracing on either side of my hips, our cocks lined up perfectly. I go to reach for them, wanting to wrap my fist around both of us together and revel in the fric-tion I honestly don't know how I lived without until now. But he smacks my hand away, shaking his head at me with a mischievous twinkle in those hazel eyes.

I spread my knees instinctively, wanting to give him a mostly stable perch, and he leans down to press a quick, soft kiss to my lips in thanks before returning to whatever he has planned. A deep groan rips from my throat when I catch on to what he's doing.

"Gonna put on a show for me, baby?"

He nods, giving me a surprisingly shy smile. I watch as he pours a generous amount of lube onto his fingers and reaches behind him. I can't see what he's doing, but I love his little hiss that turns to a groan that tells me exactly what's happening.

"You tease," I growl.

His eyes darken as he stares down at me, his pupils blown wide as he rocks back against his hand, fucking himself on his fingers to ready himself for me.

"So fucking sexy," I praise.

Unable to keep my hands to myself, I reach up and run my hands over his stomach, his chest, the fingers of one hand finding and teasing a nipple as the other trails down, dragging through the dark line of hair from his navel leading to his cock.

Realizing it's a damn crime I haven't even touched him yet, and he's already had me down his fucking throat, I let my fingers graze their way down, following his happy trail till they find his length. His cock is standing, thick and straining toward me, and just begging for my touch. Closing my fit around him, I give an experimental tug, dragging my fist from root to tip before swirling my palm over the head, mimicking how I like to do it to myself.

Callum's whole body shudders above me, and he lets out a keening whimper as he almost loses his balance and falls forward. My hand is already on his chest, pressing flat, offering him counterpressure as he regains his equilibrium.

"I take it I did something right?" I tease, grinning up at him.

"Jesus fuck, yes."

"Come here," I all but purr, sliding my hand from his

chest and up over his collarbones, circling around to tag the back of his neck and pulling him toward me for a kiss. Our mouths meet, tongues instantly tangling as I continue to explore his cock, and he writhes over me, one hand braced on my shoulder and the other twisting and working behind him.

I lose track of time as we kissed, losing myself to the feel of him against me, the smell of his skin, the taste of him. I can't get enough. Before long, Callum breaks our kiss, pressing against me to create some room.

"Enough," he gasps, surreptitiously wiping his hand on a towel I hadn't noticed him drop on the couch next to us before reaching for the foil packet now lost between the cushions. When he finds it, he quickly tears it open with his teeth and makes quick work of rolling it down my length.

I grip the base of my cock, holding it out for him like a fucking prize as he wiggles himself into position over me, but I grab his hip with my free hand, stilling his movements, needing to take back a little of the control. His eyes flash to mine, frustration blazing through their heat. "More," he gasps.

"So eager," I say, a small, teasing grin on my lips.

He rolls his eyes and groans. "Shut up and fuck me." It's more of a pleading beg than a demand. Still, it's cute as fuck and goes straight to my dick... which, for the record, agrees with him and wants nothing more than to be buried in his sweet ass that's currently hovered just above me.

"Someone's impatient," I tease.

"Someone wants your cock in his ass," he snaps.

I chuckle, leaning up to nip at his ear before intentionally dropping the tambour of my voice as low and gravely as I can manage and say, "Someone is about to get exactly what he wants."

Using my holds on his hip and my cock, I guide him

down until I feel the heat of his body pressing against the tip of my erection. Taking a deep breath and holding it, bracing for this next moment, I flex my hips slightly as I urge him lower. There is a press of resistance, an almost excruciating tightness around my crown, and I have a moment of panic that I'm going to hurt him, that he wasn't prepped enough.

He must see the moment the panic takes over because I feel the muscles of his legs tense around me, and the tight ring of muscles currently attempting to choke my cock to death press back against my invasion, and in the next breath, I feel myself breach that first ring of muscle and slide into the most perfect, scorching, delicious heat I have ever experienced.

"Oh, god," I groan, both my hands finding purchase on his hips now, and I'm not sure if it's to guide him or so I can hold on for dear life as I feel myself getting swept away.

"Fuck, you're big," he whimpers, pressing down to take another in of me into his amazing body.

"Fuck, you're tight," I moan.

He rocks slightly, and I swear I go cross-eyed. His hands are resting on my shoulders now, and he moves, fucking himself on my cock. He doesn't stop, doesn't pause again, just keeps pressing, inch after glorious inch, until his ass is flush against my hips.

I cry out, a ragged, almost tortured sound, as he engulfs the last of me. I'm overwhelmed, the sensation of his impossibly tight heat surrounding me nearly sending me over the edge.

"So good," he grunts before tensing his legs and pressing up, pulling almost all the way off me and pausing.

I brace myself, preparing for the thrust, but it doesn't come. Instead, he eases back down, taking my entire length again, my cock filling him, spreading him wide.

"Yes," I growl, my grip on his hips so tight I'm sure there

will be bruises tomorrow, but I can't find it within myself to care at the moment. I'll kiss them better in the morning. I'll kiss the damn ground he walks on if he will just keep fucking onto me like this.

He rocks his hips again, slowly at first, then faster, then with force, and before I know it, his hips are slamming down against mine as I flex up into him, meeting him thrust for thrust. I can't wrap my brain around how good it is, the feeling of him around me, his body working in perfect sync with mine as we come together.

"So good," he gasps again. His head is thrown back, arms clinging desperately to my shoulders and neck as he works himself over me, and I'm overcome.

Leaning forward, I press kisses along the column of his throat, shoulder, and that spot behind his ear. "So fucking beautiful riding my cock, taking what you need," I growl against the shell of his ear before taking the lobe between my teeth.

He cries out, his body convulsing over mine as he pleads my name. "Charlie, fuck, Charlie..."

"You close, baby?" I ask, one of my hands finding his cock between us and thumbing his slit as I wrap my fist tightly around him.

He cries out again, unintelligible babbling and noises of affirmation the only thing he can manage, apparently. Good, just the way I want him. I'm riding the razor's edge and barely able to hold on, but I want to make this last as long as possible.

"I'll take that as a yes," I chuckle, taking his mouth in a heated but brief kiss that's all tongues, teeth, and need. "Don't come yet," I instruct when I break the kiss, my hand squeezing his cock as I say it.

He whimpers, looking down at me with pleading eyes as he struggles for breath.

"Not yet," I warn, fucking up into him harder, driving us both higher.

"I can't."

"Don't you fucking come," I order, gripping the base of his cock. Judging by his pained groan, I guess I was successful in staving off his orgasm for now.

"Please," he sobs, dropping his forehead against mine as he continues to fuck himself furiously on my cock, the pleasure of his movement becoming almost too much.

"Shhh, shhh," I soothe, bringing my other hand from his hip to run down the side of his face. "Just a little longer. I'm not ready to be done."

"Please, Charlie," he pleads, and I can't resist him any longer.

"Okay, baby," I agree, releasing my hold on his cock. "Go ahead, ride my cock. Fuck me like you mean it." My hands return to his hips as he sits up straighter again, and our pace intensifies. Before long, I feel the burn of my orgasm rushing from the base of my spine, my balls pulling up tight, and I know I can't hold on any longer.

"Fuck, Cal. Come for me baby," I pant.

As if my permission had been all that was holding him back, he erupts, spilling onto my stomach and chest, my name a screaming chant on his lips.

"Fucking beautiful," I breathe, continuing to fuck up into him, my rhythm becoming erratic at the pulse and squeeze of his release around me. With a growled curse, I grip his hips and slam him down on me, burying myself to the hilt and let go, filling the condom with my release.

We collapse back against the couch, panting and sweaty.

"That was…" he begins, his breaths coming in pants against my chest as he buries his face between my pecks.

"Amazing. Mind-blowing. Fucking incredible, take your

pick," I say, struggling to catch my breath as I wrap my arms around him, unwilling to let him go just yet.

"All the above," he sighs, relaxing into my hold.

"Love the way you sound," I mumble into his hair.

"Like a maniac?" he asks, tweaking one of my nipples.

"Ouch! No! Fucking sexy as hell, dammit!" I say, letting go of him and rubbing my poor abused nipple, giving him what I hope is a disgruntled pout. Still, I have incredibly low confidence as to my control over my muscles at this point.

We lay like that, sprawled out across his couch, my fingers tracing lazy patterns across his back, with Callum tucked securely against my chest. His head rests on my shoulder while he toys with my chest hair in a surprisingly intimate and comforting gesture.

It hits me that I have never experienced a moment like this before. Whenever I have been with women in the past, one or both of us always either scurried off to clean up right away, or if we did stay and cuddle for a bit, they would either rather spoon in the bed or complain about my chest hair getting itchy after only a few minutes. But this quiet contentment I feel wrapping around Callum and I has a sense of peace settling into my bones.

I could get used to this.

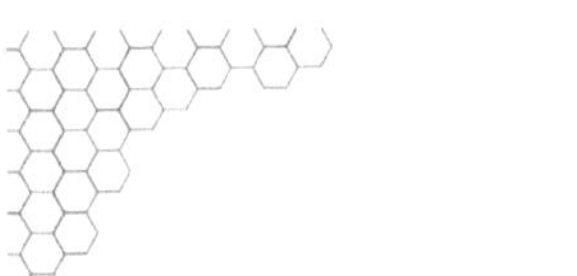

CHAPTER SIXTEEN

CALLUM

The next morning, with the sun streaming in through the window, warming the bed, I wake up alone. For a moment, a brief, terrified moment, I think I might have dreamed the entire exchange from the night before... the dinner and easy conversation, the playful back and forth when we got home, and the absolutely mind-blowing, life-altering sex. I couldn't have dreamed it all, right? There is no way my imagination is that good.

But then the smell hits me... Bacon and coffee. A wide smile breaks across my face, and I don't even try to hide it.

Rolling onto my back, I take a lazy stretch, enjoying the aches and pains, the pleasant soreness that only comes from a body getting well and thoroughly used. After that first epic round on the couch, we peeled ourselves apart, literally, thanks to the cold and sticky leftovers of the mess I made of his chest. We stumbled into my shower, barely keeping our hands and mouths to ourselves long enough to rinse off before exchanging mind-bending steamy blowjobs. You know, I gotta hand it to Charlie. For it being his first time sucking cock, he took me like a champ, and I swear he sucked my soul outta the tip of my dick. After the mutual shower blow jobs, we managed to refuel and hydrate while pretending to watch something on Netflix like we had originally intended, but sitting next to Charlie, both of us only in our boxers, was not conducive to either of us paying any attention to whatever was going on on the screen.

Eventually, we tumbled into my bed for round two before passing out tangled together under the sheet. I would say it was the best night's sleep I've had in possibly ever, but I'm not sure if it counts as a full night's sleep if we each woke the other one up at least twice for some mix of making out like teenager, heavy petting, and another round of mutual orgasms until we both officially zonked out around 4 am.

Yep. Best night ever, even if sleep wasn't really involved.

Giving myself one last deep stretch, feeling a few satisfying pops in my back and hip, I finally roll out of bed in search of the source of the heavenly smell. Not bothering to find clothes since there wasn't anyone home I needed to worry about hiding from, I give myself permission to enjoy the rare freedom and pad down the hall and into the kitchen, still naked, where Charlie is busy cooking.

I can't hold back the laugh that bubbles out of me when I round the corner and see he, too, is still naked, except for a ridiculous apron with the image of a hairy chest screen printed on it that my sister gave me for Christmas a few years ago.

"Hey, beautiful," he says, turning toward me when he hears my laugh and flashing me a quick smile.

"Morning," I reply, stepping into the kitchen to kiss him, just a brief, chaste peck on the cheek.

"Wait, is beautiful alright? Is that not something guys like?" The look of earnest concern on his face is ridiculously endearing, and I can't help but lean in and press another soft kiss to his lips.

"It's great. Can't say I've ever been called that before, but not sure I mind it either," I answer with a grin, giving his ass a light slap as I step back to lean against the counter. He heaves a sigh of relief, the tension visibly leaving his shoulders as he flashes me another smile.

"Sleep well?" he asks, turning back to the pan he's minding on the stove.

"Yeah, really good," I answer. "Better than I can remember, actually. That is, once this horny asshole next to me finally wore us both out and let me sleep," I say with a wink.

A blush creeps up his chest and neck and blooms on his cheeks at my teasing, and it's fascinating to watch his skin flush like that, being able to track the progress across the expanse of his bare chest. Shit, I better get a handle on my wayward thoughts before other things start waking up for the morning, and we ruin breakfast by getting distracted.

"Good," he says through a shy smile before handing me a cup of coffee.

I accept it and take a sip, savoring the rich, deep, and slightly sweet flavor of a perfectly brewed cup. Black, one sugar. Exactly how I like it.

"How'd you know how I like my coffee?" I ask, a little surprised.

"Just a lucky guess," he chuckles. "Now go sit. I'm making you breakfast."

"Yessir," I reply with a grin.

"Oh, don't start that now. I refuse to burn this bacon, dammit."

He's a fan of 'sir.' Noted.

I do as instructed and settle in at the table, sipping my coffee and waiting for the caffeine to kick in and wash away the remnants of sleep fog still clinging to the edges of my brain. A few minutes later, Charlie sets a plate in front of me loaded with eggs, bacon, two pancakes, and some toast, along with a matching plate for him.

"Jesus Christ, I'm not going to be able to move today if you keep feeding me like this," I joke.

"Sorry," he says, a sheepish smile tugging at the corner of his lips. "I got a little excited and carried away."

"I thought that was last night?" I say with a wink. "No, it's great, just more than I was expecting."

"Well, that too," he laughs, sitting down across from me and digging into his own meal.

After a few bites, both of us were quiet as we let the food and coffee do their job and wake us the rest of the way up. I put down my fork and look up at him, my expression serious. "Listen," I say.

"Uh-oh," he groans. "That doesn't sound good."

"No, no," I laugh, realizing how that must have come across. "Nothing bad. I just want to thank you."

"Thank me? For what?"

"For last night," I reply, lowering my eyes.

"Oh! You mean for the epic dicking!" he laughs.

"I'm trying to be serious, you dick!" I scold through a laugh.

"It was a great night," he agrees, his tone and expression genuine.

"I've... I've never done anything like that before," I confess, unable to look directly at him, instead studying my plate.

"What? The anal? I swear you said you had!" he exclaims, a note of panic in his voice.

"No, not the sex. Of course, I have. I already told you that," I correct him, shaking my head.

"Oh, you mean sleeping together afterward?"

"Exactly. I've never really done that," I say, painfully aware of the heat filling my cheeks as I blush.

"Sleep with someone?" he asks, confirming.

"Well, yeah," I chuckle.

"What about Georgie's mom? Didn't you guys sleep together when you were dating or married or whatever?"

"Never married. And sure, I guess, but that was different," I say, unsure of exactly how to explain this.

"How so?"

"We weren't… connected," I say, finally looking up at him. "Like, we were together because of something, because of Georgie. It was more like convenience than anything."

"What do you mean?" he asks, the wrinkle of confusion between his brows proving I am doing a horrible job explaining myself.

"We were both young, and I was stupid. I knocked her up on a one-night stand in a club bathroom. Classy, I know. I honestly hadn't expected to see her again, but she tracked me down when she found out she was pregnant. We decided to give it a go and have the kid together, give it a shot for Georgie's sake. And the rest, they say, is history. We went through the motions for a while, but it didn't take long before we both realized it would never work out. Then one day, out of the blue, with no notice, she just packed up her shit and left. Came home to find a stack of papers on the counter that signed over all her legal rights to Georgie as a parent. Haven't seen or heard from her since." I hadn't intended to tell him all of that, not yet, at least, but it just spilled out once I got going. I can't deny it feels good to have it out there, though.

"Shit, Callum. How'd Georgie handle that? I can't imagine anyone walking away from that little girl," Charlie says.

I swear I feel my heart actually melt and hear a resounding crack of the walls I have built up around that part of myself when I hear his words. After everything I said, and even after everything we did last night... his first thought was for Georgie. Fuck, I am such a goner.

"Thankfully, she hardly remembers her mother at this point. She left when Georgie was three, so she didn't have many memories from that time in general. Every once in a while, she asks why it's just the two of us when so many of her friends have two parents, but it's never been a real issue for her."

"You two make a good team."

Seriously, it should be illegal for gorgeous, sexy men to say sweet shit like that while we are both sitting naked. I'm not supposed to fight off tears while my dick is out, dammit!

We both turn back to our food, each putting away another good portion of the meal before I notice the line between his brows hasn't eased and there's a tension in his shoulders that wasn't there before.

"Penny for your thoughts?" I ask, nudging his leg with my toes under the table.

He doesn't look up at me, but I see his back and shoulders expand with a deep breath before I hear him ask, barely above a whisper. "What if things don't work out? What happens then?"

Oh, my heart. This fucking man.

"This is different, Charlie," I say, reaching across the table and placing my hand on top of his where it rests next to his plate like he wanted to reach out but hadn't quite worked up the courage yet. "I'm not just saying that, or placating you. This... whatever this is between us... This is real. I've never felt this way about anyone before." God, I hope that doesn't scare him off, but after everything that's happened in the last twelve hours, I couldn't hold back if I tried.

"Me either," he confesses, a shy smile on his lips.

"Don't worry about what might happen or the what ifs. Enjoy what's happening now."

"Just let it happen," he says, like he's quoting something. I watch as he sorts through something in his mind before he heaves a deep sigh and finally looks up at me fully, a bright smile on his face. "And what is happening now, by the way?"

Hello, whiplash, but I just roll with it.

"Right now, you are finishing your breakfast, and then joining me in the shower."

"And why are we going to the shower?" he asks, grinning at me.

"Because I think you are very, very dirty after a night of exertion and need a lot of… scrubbing," I tease with a ridiculous eyebrow waggle.

"Oh, is that right?" he asks, playing along.

"Absolutely," I say, my grin turning downright lascivious.

"Anything in particular we should pay extra attention to?"

"I can think of a few things, actually. In fact, I think only one thing can reach these particular spots and do a… thorough enough job."

"I see," he says, having to clear his throat as his eyes darken. "And what might that be?"

"My tongue," I respond, my eyes sparking with heat. His eyes blow wide at my answer and he really does choke this time, needing to take a swing of coffee before he can settle down and meet my gaze again. All I can do is chuckle. He's so damn fun to rile up, especially when I know I get to reap the rewards.

"Finish your breakfast, Charlie. We have a couple more hours before I need to pick up Georgie from your mom, and I intend to make good use of every minute of them. You're going to need your strength."

"Is that a threat or a promise?" he asks around a mouthful as he shovels the last of his food into his mouth.

"Both," I wink.

CHAPTER SEVENTEEN

CHARLIE

Two hours and at least as many orgasms later, Callum and I finally lay, spent, in the center of his bed, catching our breath from yet another round of earth-shattering sex. For a guy who had never even touched a dick until last night, I sure can't seem to get enough of it now. Everything about the man currently snoring gently against my chest draws me in, sinking its claws in and not letting go.

His rhythmic breathing is a reminder of the intensity of last night and this morning. It was so much more than just physical; there was a connection, a spark that ignited something within me that I never knew existed. Not until him. But as the sex haze slowly clears from my mind, the questions that have been bubbling beneath the surface roll in.

The clock on the nightstand ticks away, each second a reminder of reality closing in on the little bubble we created around ourselves over the last twelve hours, closing in and ready to make it burst. The question is, will we still be standing when it does, and the dust settles? Will I?

I try to calm my thoughts and live in the moment,

soaking up the last few minutes of the quiet with him in my arms before we have to return to the real world outside these four walls. Callum has to pick up Georgie in less than an hour, and I made the excuse of having some errands to run while we talked about our plans for the day between the second round of shower blow jobs and the third round in the bed... or was it the fourth? Either way, I pulled what feels like a chicken shit move and begged off going with him to pick up Georgie. It's not that I don't want to spend time with them, because I do, I really do. It's just that I need a moment to process the tidal wave of feelings that's taken over my mind and heart.

Twenty minutes later, Callum's alarm goes off, signaling the end of our little escape and our inevitable return to the real world. We chat easily as we each throw on some clothes and head out to the living room to find the pieces that got tossed around in our rush to get undressed last night. As Callum digs through the couch cushions for his keys, I can't help but glance at the pictures on the wall—Callum and Georgie laughing on a beach somewhere, another of them all bundled up in full winter gear with a snow-covered mountain in the background, another one that's clearly in front of Georgie's school here in Rapids Bay... all of them featuring both father and daughter, arms wrapped around each other, their smiles genuine and infectious. It hits me that this isn't just about Callum and me; it's about Georgie too. They're a package deal, and I need to figure out if I'm ready for all of it.

The chilly morning air greets us as we step outside and exchange a quick, sweet goodbye on the front step of his building. We exchange innocent kisses and promises to see each other later before turning to our cars and heading out. But instead of driving home or accomplishing one of the errands I have been putting off, I find myself driving toward the hardware store a couple of blocks off Main Street. My dad's shop was like a second home for us boys growing up, and something inside me is longing for the familiar right now... and my dad. Dad has always been the one I turn to when life gets a bit too complicated, and right now, I need his perspective more than ever.

The bell above the door chimes as I push it open and step into the warmth of the shop. Dad looks up from the catalog he was flipping through behind the counter and waves me over with a warm smile.

"Hey Charlie, what's up?" he asks.

I manage a weak smile as I walk closer. "Hey, Dad. Can we talk?"

He snaps the catalog on the counter closed and gestures for me to follow him into the back. When we get to his office, he flips on the monitor for the little camera he has pointed at the shop door so he can watch people coming in and gestures for me to sit. "Alright, spill. What's on your mind?"

I take a deep breath, exhaling slowly. "So, you remember Callum, right?" He nods, patiently waiting for me to get to the point. "Yeah, well, we um... fuck, this is weird to talk to you about..." I say, questioning if coming here was a good idea.

"Spit it out, son. I've yet to hear a single thing outta any of the five of you boys that surprises me. Just say what you need to say."

"Yeah, okay. Fair enough. So, Callum and I spent the night together last night, and I can't stop thinking about it."

Dad leans back in his chair, studying me. "And this is a bad thing because?"

"Because it's never been like this before. I've never been with a guy, and now it's like... I can't deny there's something more here, but I don't know if I'm ready for it."

He chuckles, shaking his head. "Charlie, I love you, but

you've always been the one to leap before you look, take the stupid chance, and hope for the best. So what's different now?" I open my mouth to respond, but he holds his hand up to cut me off. "Don't answer that. Just think about it. Look, change is scary, especially when it's something new. But that's what makes life interesting. So, spill, what's the real issue here?"

I glance at the security camera feed and watch a display sign in front of the window flutter in the current generated by the central heat as I sort through my thoughts. "Callum's an amazing guy, dad. I've never felt this way before. But it's like I'm not just falling for him—I'm falling for his whole life. Georgie's a sweetheart, and I can't help but wonder if I'm ready for all of it. I mean, being a part of their lives in a more permanent way, hell, potentially as another dad figure. Am I crazy for thinking about this stuff after just a month?"

Dad leans forward, his eyes serious. "Charlie, you're over-thinking this. Sure, it's a big step, but you won't know if you're ready until you try. Every new parent says that... that you never know if you are ready until it actually happens. You think your mother and I had any idea what we were doing when we had you? You think I felt 'ready' when Barbie told me she was pregnant with you? Not a chance in hell. No one is ever 'ready.' I promise you Callum wasn't ready before she was born, but you'd have to be deaf, blind, and dumb not to see how that little girl is the center of his world. And besides, I have seen you with her. You're amazing with Georgie; she has you wrapped so tightly around her little finger. It's fucking adorable. Maybe you are looking at this all wrong. What if Georgie isn't the package the rest needs to fit in, but instead, she just might be the missing piece of the puzzle?"

I nod, taking in his words. "But what if I mess up? What if

I'm not cut out for this kind of commitment? I don't want to hurt them."

I look up and see a soft expression on my dad's face as he answers. "Charlie, you've never been the type to hurt anyone intentionally. You care about people; it's what you do. And it's clear you care about Callum. Just take it one day at a time. But I will tell you this... the fact you are even asking that question and have that worry tells me all I need to know."

As I sit there, letting my father's words sink in, I realize he's right. Life is full of uncertainties, and sometimes, you just have to take a leap of faith. It may be a big step, but I know I want to take it with Callum and, by extension, Georgie.

Dad and I shoot the shit for a little while longer before I make my excuses and head out, leaving with a promise to bring Callum and Georgie over for dinner again sometime soon. After my heart-to-heart with my dad, I decide its time to confront my fears and stop running away from what I truly want. I drive back to Callum's place, my mind buzzing with a newfound determination.

Betha is just arriving home with an armload of groceries, and being the good midwestern boy like my momma raised me, I take the bag from her and help her inside... all while being berated that she isn't an invalid and can do it her damn self. Once inside, I tell her I really just needed an excuse to get in the building and give her a kiss on the cheek and a wink before taking the stairs up to Callum's apartment two at a time.

Stopping outside his door, I take a deep breath and steel resolve for the conversation I know I want and need to have. I knock and wait impatiently for someone to answer. Are they still not back? Fuck, I should have called or texted first. I turn to head back down the stairs after only waiting a grand total of thirty seconds, even though those were the longest thirty seconds in the history of the world, before I hear the door open behind me.

"Charlie?" Callum asks, and I can hear the smile in his voice before I even turn around. Fuck, just hearing him calms something inside me, helping my head to clear and reminding me why I'm here. I turn back around and offer him a grin and an awkward wave.

"What brings you back? Did you forget something?"

I take a deep breath, looking directly into Callum's eyes. "I wanted to see you. And maybe spend some time with Georgi,e if she'll have me."

Callum's smile widens, his eyes sparking with a mix of emotions I can't quite place as he nods toward Georgie, who's peeking out from behind the door. "What do you say, troublemaker? Want to spend some time with Charlie?"

Georgie's face lights up, and she hops out from behind the door. She nods enthusiastically, sending her curls bouncing around her head. "Yes, please!"

As we spend the day together—playing board games, making silly faces at one another whenever Callum turns his back, and telling increasingly horrible puns just to make each other laugh—I realize that maybe, just maybe, this is the right step for me. Love, commitment, and a family might not be as daunting as I once thought.

Eventually, the sun hangs low in the sky, casting a warm glow over the three of us as we sit on the living room floor, an intense game of Uno spread out on the coffee table. I steal a glance at Callum, and he catches my eye, a silent under-standing passing between us.

Maybe it's too soon to say the words out loud, but as I look at the makeshift little family in front of me, I can't help but feel that love has a funny way of finding you when you least expect it.

And as Georgie giggles, her laughter echoing through the

room, I know that taking a chance on love, on Callum, on this unconventional family, might just be the best decision I've ever made. Life is full of uncertainties, but sometimes, all you need is a little courage and a whole lot of heart to navigate those unknowns and come out the other side with everything you never knew you wanted.

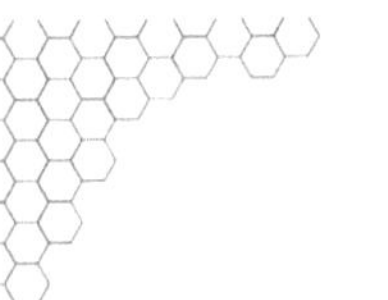

CHAPTER EIGHTEEN

CALLUM

In the week since that first night together and the next day spent hanging out with Georgie, Charlie has been a daily part of our lives in one way or another. Between working together, sneaking little moments away when we can, and Charlie joining us for as many dinners as he can manage, it's been… a dream.

Never in a million years would I have expected things to turn out like this when Georgie and I first pulled into town and what I thought was the local screw-up rammed into our car. I couldn't have been more wrong. Charlie isn't a screwup, far from it. There are very few things that man can't do, and do amazingly on the first try. He's just eager and earnest, and to some people, that may feel like he's coming on too strong, but I thank whatever powers that be every day that this crazy man decided to direct that focus and attention on Georgie and me.

While we have spent as much time as possible with Georgie, I won't lie and say we haven't also been sneaking off every chance we get to fool around, or just straight-up fuck.

The man is insatiable, and I'm not far behind as far as my incessant need for him goes. I can't get enough.

Which is why I am surprised, and not ashamed to admit a little disappointed, that we find ourselves in Charlie's truck after dropping Georgie off for another girl's day with his mom and *not* heading back to one of our places. I had fully expected to spend our Georgie-free day naked and wrapped around him in more ways than one.

"You're really not going to tell me where we're going?" I ask again, unsure if I'm more curious or annoyed at the situation.

"Nope," he says with a grin, popping the p obnoxiously. "But we're almost there, so keep your pants on."

"Really? Usually, you're the one growling at me to get them off," I reply with a smirk. He barks out a laugh, his hand coming to rest high on my thigh as he takes another turn out of town. A few minutes later, we come up to a fenced-in parking lot with a large warehouse on the far enough that backs up to the woods beyond. There's a sign hanging on the fence near the entrance.

"Paintball? Seriously?"

"Yep!" he declares. "It's Donnie's birthday tomorrow, and this is what he wanted to do this year. Years ago, all of us brothers decided we were tired of the overblown parties mom always tried to throw, so we got together and swore to always pick something fun to do together instead. Playing the brotherly bonding card keeps mom off our backs."

"That's actually really smart. Sarah and I should have started something like that years ago," I say.

"So, want to go?" he asks, looking like an excited little kid almost bouncing out of his seat.

"Of course I do," I reply, laughing. He pulls into the lot and finds a parking spot between Donnie's immaculately restored vintage truck, Alfie's honest-to-God Mini Cooper, and Ollie's motorcycle. Seeing all four vehicles lined up together is maybe the most accurate description of the Larson brothers I could possibly imagine. There's another brother somewhere in the mix, Eddie, but he's off on a several-month-long contract for work, and I haven't met him yet.

The five of us walk through the entrance doors at one end of the warehouse. This first section is blocked off from the rest and built out into a lobby area and locker room. A wall of thick-paned windows looked out over the course, taking up the rest of the massive building.

"Hey guys, welcome. There's a game in session right now, but it's winding down," the guy working the front door told us by way of a greeting.

Donnie stepped forward and got us checked in before we were directed to the locker rooms around the corner. "We've got protective gear and masks. Make sure you get suited up before your session starts."

We all nod and head off to change while we wait for the other group to wrap up. There's a bathroom area with a row of stalls and a big room full of lockers. I take a quick look around at the other four getting ready, noticing the various gear offered and what each of the brothers are using, taking stock.

Judging by the detailed explanation Charlie was diving into as we all suited up, I can tell he assumes I am new to this. Well, you know what they say about people who assume. Little does he know that I not only competed in a paintball league back in high school and college, my team coming out on top in several high-ranking tournaments over the course of the almost six years we competed together. Not only that, but my dad and uncle were military men who took their guns seriously. I've been hunting since I was big enough to carry a rifle.

This was going to be fun.

And if Charlie was going to insist on explaining how to pull the damn trigger on the (rather shoddy) paintball guns this place provides, then what he doesn't know won't hurt him… yet. I quickly decide it will be more fun to play along with his assumptions for now.

Once we are all suited up and ready to go, we head back out to the lobby as a group.

"So, have you guys been here before?" the guy at the front desk asks as he leads us to the door that opens into the course.

"Some of us have," Donnie answers, smiling.

Seeing an opening, I can't resist playing up the clueless act a bit. "How does this work, exactly? Do we just go against each other, or what? Are there teams?" I ask, trying my best to sound confused and unsure.

"Nah, there's not enough people for teams. You'll go in at two-minute intervals, giving you a chance to spread out. When the horn sounds… try to stay alive," the guy explains.

"Stay alive?" I laugh. "That doesn't sound ominous at all."

"Don't worry, man," Ollie says, chuckling. "We'll go easy on you."

"You scared?" Alfie asks, nudging me with his elbow good-naturedly.

"Nope," I say with a grin. "Let's go," I reply.

"Let's let the newbie go first… give him a head start," Donnie suggests. Clearly, Alfie and Donnie still haven't gotten over their issue with me since the hazing incident weeks ago. That's just going to make this even more fun.

Fifteen minutes later, I've taken out Ollie, Alfie, and Donnie with little to no effort. Ollie was the first to go; a quick shot to the shin as he strolled past my hiding spot was all it took. It took him a moment to find where I was crouching behind a stack of paint-splattered barrels, and when I shot him a wink, he burst out laughing.

"Knew not to trust that look in your eyes back there. Let me guess, you're some kind of sniper or some shit, aren't you?" he asked.

"Something like that," I said with a smile and a shrug.

That earned another laugh from Ollie before he saluted me and said, "Give 'em hell," before heading back to the safe zone.

Alfie and Donnie were even more entertaining to take down. Alfie had taken up a spot behind a half wall and hadn't noticed Donnie sneaking up on him. Two quick shots later, I had taken them both down before either knew what hit them.

"Fuck!" Alfie screeched, trying to reach the spot on the center of his back where my shot landed. "Dammit, Donnie! Sneaking up on me like a little bitch? Really?"

"Wasn't me, asshole. Got me too," Donnie griped, rubbing at his shoulder that took a solid shot.

Three down. One to go.

While I could easily take him down quickly, like the others, I think I'm more in the mood to play with my prey a little before going for the takedown.

It doesn't take long to find Charlie sneaking his way through a maze of scrap metal and car parts. I don't think he realizes it's just the two of us left, so I step out from my cover and hiss to get his attention. "Psst. Charlie!" I whisper-shout at him.

His head snaps up, and I see him hesitate for a moment, clearly trying to decide if he wants to shoot me or not. He's too damn cute... and naïve.

"Hey, babe," he finally says, shooting me a grin and

lowering his rifle. I step closer and have to bite my tongue to keep from laughing out loud.

"Hey, seen anyone?" I ask.

"Not yet. I think I heard a few shots, but not sure who's still alive or out," he answers, scanning the area around us.

"Do we have a plan?" I ask, feigning looking around and searching for his brothers.

"This way. Donnie usually plants himself over in that corner. We can pick him off first," Charlie says, turning away from me and starting to walk away. Unable to help myself, I reach out and slap his ass before he's taken more than a step.

"Fuck, Cal! What was that for?" he asks, reaching a hand back to cover his ass protectively. So fuckin cute.

"Serves you right for taunting me like that. Your ass is fucking biteable in those jeans," I all but groan. It's true. His ass does look damn fine, and I can't wait to get my hands on it when we get out of here. "Besides, I think we should go this way. Think I heard something," I say, motioning off to my right, not giving him a chance to respond.

"You lead the way, and I'll watch your back," Charlie offers.

I grin and nod, only about forty percent sure he won't take the cheap shot and shoot me in the back. We start moving through the course, and I pretend to keep an eye out for movement, making an exaggerated show of looking around. We're no more than twenty feet from where I found him when the first touch of cool fingers slipping into the waistband of my pants catches me off guard.

"Charlie, cut it out," I scold, with absolutely zero conviction behind the words.

"Come on, Cal. Please? I'm bored."

Hell yes. If he's already getting handsy, it won't be long before he drags us back to town and behind closed doors again so we can continue with the plans I had for the day originally. Though, where's the fun in giving in that easily?

"Just stay focused. We can fool around later," I tell him.

The heat of his body blankets my back as he steps closer and leans in to whisper in my ear. "I'd rather fuck you right now. How about we go to the truck, and I eat you out and then bend you over the tailgate and pound your tight hole until you can't see straight?"

"Fuck, Charlie," I groan, already feeling my cock swelling at his words.

"Yeah, that's the idea," he laughs, sliding his fingers farther into my pants, teasing the crease of my ass through my boxers.

"Later, Charlie. Come on," I respond, attempting to actually be the voice of reason now. If he keeps that up, I know I'll be on my knees for him right here in the middle of the course, his brothers, the front desk guy, and any cameras be damned.

"You're no fun," he pouts, pulling his hand free.

"Yep, that's me, fun sucker," I deadpan.

"Pretty sure you're better at sucking something else," he teases, pressing in close behind me, letting me feel the bulge of his erection against my ass. I'm not sure how much longer I can keep this up. I'm going to have to take him down soon... so I can go down on him not long after.

"Maybe, if you're good and we can get out of here quickly, you can convince me to let you top me when we get home," he whispers into my neck, his hot breath tickling the little bit of skin visible between my gear.

"Seriously?" I croak, my mouth dry and knees weak at his words. We've been going at it like a couple of sex-crazed demon rabbits since our first night together and have done pretty much anything and everything either of us could dream up. But he hasn't been ready to be on the receiving end of full-on penetration yet. Honestly, until he offered it up to me like that just now, I didn't think that was something I even really wanted from him, but now it's the only thing I can think of.

"Yes," he growls, grinding against my ass one more time before stepping away from me. "Now, let's finish the game."

"I'm gonna hold you to that," I warn. He's gonna be pissed when he realizes I played him as far as this game goes, but fuck if I am going to let a round of paintball come between us like that.

"I hope you do," he says, blowing me a kiss before turning and walking away. Seeing my chance, I take it once he's sufficiently far away that I know the shot won't actually hurt, maybe just bruise a little, but nothing serious.

"Fuck!" Charlie screeches, his hand going to his ass to cover the mark my shot just made, covering his right asscheek.

"What the hell, Cal?" he asks, eyes blazing when he turns back to me.

"Sorry, babe. That was too easy," I laugh, unable to hold it back any longer.

"Yeah, yeah, very funny," he grumbles, shaking his head.

"Aw, come on. You can't be mad. It was a clean shot," I soothe, quickly walking over to him, brushing his hand away, and taking over rubbing the spot for him.

"I can, and I am," he replies, trying to pout, but the smile he's unable to hide kind of ruins the effect.

"Don't be mad, Charlie," I say, wrapping the arm not holding my gun around his waist and pulling him close.

"I'm not, really, just surprised," he chuckles.

"Really?" I ask.

"Yes, really," he answers, wrapping his free arm around my waist, mirroring my hold on him for a moment. "Come on. We've gotta find the others and end this stupid game so I can get you home and make you pay for that little stunt," he laughs, stepping back.

"Oh, that? Yeah. They're already out," I say with a shrug.

"All of them?" he asks, stunned.

"Yep," I answer, popping the p.

"But... how?"

Deciding to finally let him in on the joke, I reach my hand out for a shake. "Hi, name's Callum. Six-time Rocky Mountain Paintball League champion."

His eyes pop open comically wide, and his jaw drops for a second before he bursts out laughing, dropping his gun and throwing his head back, letting the sound fill the warehouse. "Jesus fuck, Cal. And you just let us make asses of ourselves like that?" he asks through his laughs.

"Y'all were having such a fun time mansplaining the shit out of it. I just didn't have the heart to stop you," I chuckle.

"Touche," he replies. "Fine, Mr. World Champ or whatever... let's get out of here and have our own little award ceremony." He throws me a wink over his shoulder before he bends down and picks up his discarded gun, firing off a round that connects with my shin with a painful sting.

"Fucker," I hiss through gritted teeth. "You are so paying for that later."

"Hope so," he says with a wink before taking off toward the entrance and his brothers at a run.

CHAPTER NINETEEN

CHARLIE

’m already rock fucking hard by the time I slam my apartment door shut behind us and push Callum up against the wall, crushing my lips to his. There's nothing sweet or romantic about it; it's pure need and desire and want. And the fact he's been teasing me all damn day with those tight fucking jeans and the way they hug his ass and cock has left me on edge since before we even got to the paintball range. He'd known exactly what he was doing, and I can't wait to bury my cock in his ass and show him exactly what he does to me.

The taste of whiskey is strong on his breath as I shove my tongue into his mouth, twining with his in a dance we have perfected over the last few weeks. The warmth of his mouth, the groan he lets out as he tastes me, only adds fuel to my fire.

I had wanted to get him home immediately after his little stunt at paintball this afternoon, but my brothers convinced us to go out for a drink with them first, and we couldn't exactly say no since we were technically there to celebrate Donnie's birthday. Fucking cockblock.

My hands move along the hard lines of his chest, slipping beneath the tight material of his shirt to graze my fingertips over his stomach, teasing into his happy trail. I tug the rest of the shirt out of his waistband and pull away from the kiss, yanking the shirt over his head and tossing it to the floor.

"Fuck," I growl, my fingers trailing over the lines of his pecs, tangling in the coarse hair there. "I love your body."

And I do. Looking at him now, I don't know how I ever could have questioned my attraction to him. There's nothing soft or delicate about him. He's all firm muscles, coarse hair, and hard lines. I can't get enough. I always want to be touching him, feeling him, tasting him. It's taken no time at all for me to go from assuming I was straight to being completely addicted to everything about this man.

"So take advantage of it," he replies, his voice a low, raspy purr.

I don't need further invitation. I grab the back of his neck, dragging him closer and kissing him again. Our bodies press together, and the heat that radiates from his skin sears my flesh everywhere we are connected.

"I'm gonna fuck you until you can't stand straight for a week," I murmur, my hand sliding between us to grip the outline of his dick through his jeans.

"Fuck, you're so fucking hot," he groans.

"Get on your knees," I growl into the kiss, my lips brushing his as they form the words. "I want that pretty little mouth of yours wrapped around my cock."

He grins as he pulls away from my hold. "As you wish." He drops to his knees, unfastening my pants and tugging them down as he goes.

I reach for the hem of my shirt and yank it over my head, tossing it aside as I watch him peel my boxer briefs down my legs, my cock springing free and almost smacking him in the forehead in the process.

"Damn," he all but moans, reaching up to stroke the length of my cock. "Someone's been looking forward to this."

"Shut up and suck it," I say, my voice more gravel than anything at this point.

"Oh, demanding, I like it." His fingers curl around my shaft, squeezing firmly as his tongue slides up the underside to swirl around the tip.

"Fucking hell," I gasp, gripping his hair, pulling him closer, and pressing my cock against his lips. He opens for me, sliding his lips around my girth and taking me deep into his throat in one fluid move.

"Fuck," I grunt, holding him against me for a moment, his nose brushing against the base of my cock. I feel him swallow around me, and the sensation sends shivers of pleasure rushing through my body.

He pulls back against my hold after another beat, his mouth coming off me with a pop. "How do you want me?" he asks, his voice harsh through his wrecked throat and eyes bright with the few tears that sprang up as he took me deep.

"On your feet. Turn around. Hands on the wall."

He hums his agreement as he rises, stripping out of his clothes in record time before turning and planting his palms on the wall, legs spread.

I grab the packet of lube and condom from my wallet in my discarded pants and make quick work of suiting up before tearing open the lube packet with my teeth and squirting a generous amount onto my fingers.

"Do you have any idea how badly I've wanted you tonight?" I ask, stepping closer against his back and nipping at the back of his neck.

"About as much as I've wanted you," he pants, pressing his ass back against me.

"Good, then you won't mind if I'm a little rough." He

whimpers at my words as I run a finger between his cheeks, circling his hole.

He moans, his hips rocking back. "Give me everything you've got."

"Careful what you wish for," I say. Something about his challenge has me changing my plans slightly. I drop to my knees behind him, quickly wiping my hand off on my discarded jeans before spreading his cheeks with my hands and diving in with my tongue.

"Holy shit," he groans, his hips bucking backward.

I've been on the receiving end of this particular pleasure several times in the last week or so but have never taken the chance to indulge and just can't resist any longer. I lick and tease his entrance, alternating between broad, flat swipes and flicks of my tongue around the rim.

"You're gonna drive me crazy," he says, his words breathy and strained above me.

"Good," I growl against his skin.

"Charlie, fuck, I need more."

"Patience," I chide, pressing a kiss against him before nipping lightly with my teeth, causing his knees to buckle slightly.

"Not my strong suit," he bites out through what sounds like gritted teeth.

"I know," I grin. Sliding my thumbs into his crease, I spread him wider and begin working my tongue deeper.

"Jesus," he pants, slamming a fist against the wall. "Please, Charlie. I need more."

"Oh, I know, but I'm not going to give it to you yet," I say, my tone deceptively casual as I continue to press kisses and nips around his hole.

"Fucker," he snaps.

I pull back and slap his ass, digging my fingers into the

fleshy mound. He moans at the move, his hips jerking back toward me like they are searching for more.

"Like that, huh?" I chuckle.

"Yes," he admits.

"More?" I ask, leaning in to give him another firm lick.

"God, yes."

I spank him again, harder, and the sound echoes through the kitchen. Callum cries out, his back arching.

"Such a good boy," I coo, pressing a kiss to the rapidly blooming handprint on his asscheek.

"Yeah, now show me what a good man does," he challenges.

"Oh, I plan to," I say, standing and reaching for another packet of lube and coating my fingers again. I swear we both have them stashed everywhere and anywhere at this point. Never know when you might need one in a pinch.

"Then what are you waiting for?"

"Nothing," I say, slipping a finger inside him. He arches against me, pressing back against my invasion with a gasp.

"Finally," he says with a sigh. I chuckle, sliding a second finger in alongside the first.

The sounds he makes, the whimpers, pants, and needy pleading sighs, only serve to drive my need for him higher as I work him open, my cock desperate to be inside him.

"Like that, hm?" I tease as I wrap my other hand around my sheathed cock, needing to stave off the orgasm I already feel churning beneath the surface.

"Oh, fuck yeah. Give me more," he pleads.

I press a third finger inside as he rocks back against me again, meeting my push.

"Greedy," I chuckle, pressing kisses to the back of his neck and across his shoulder.

"Damn straight."

Unwilling to deprive either of us any longer, I pull my

hand from his body and replace it with the head of my cock, pressing against his prepped rim and sliding in easily. We let out matching moans as I press in to the hilt in one long, smooth thrust.

"Fuck me hard," he begs, his voice wrecked.

"My pleasure," I whisper before pulling my hips back and sliding almost all the way out of him. My hands find his hips, fingers digging in, and I feel a shiver run through him, and I tighten my hold further, holding him still. I pause like that for a moment, making him wait before I slam back into him, hard. His responding groan is low and desperate and music to my ears.

"God, you're so fucking perfect," I praise, starting a slow but hard rhythm of pulling back slowly before slamming home. Again and again, slow and hard, slow and hard, driving us both higher with each thrust.

"Harder," he begs.

"So demanding," I chuckle, not giving him what he wants, maintaining the same intense rhythm.

"Damit," he hisses, attempting to push back against me.

I smack his hip lightly in warning. "You're enjoying this, and you know it," I chide, punctuating my point with another hard thrust.

"Shut up. More. I need more. Wanna cum," he babbles.

"Shh," I soothe, running my hands from his hips, over his back and shoulders.

"God, Charlie, fuck me. Make me scream."

I lean forward, my lips brushing the shell of his ear. "Relax, Cal."

"Ugh, please. Please. I'm so close. I need..."

"Need what? Tell me," I coax, pressing a kiss behind his ear. "Tell me what you need."

"I need... I..." he stutters, unable to find the words as I keep up my infuriating pace.

"Tell me," I prompt again, taking his lobe between my teeth with a teasing nip.

"Your cock," he pants.

"You have that."

"Faster, harder, just… ugh."

His body is vibrating beneath me, the entire length of our bodies pressed together from chest to thighs as I keep up my steady pace, angling my hips to make sure I hit his prostate with each thrust.

"I hate you," he growls, his head falling back against my shoulder.

"No, you don't," I laugh, pressing a kiss to the side of his throat, now on delicious display for me. I can't resist sliding a hand up and around to grasp the front of his throat as I straighten, pulling him with me and keeping his head on my shoulder. "Now breathe," I whisper against his cheek.

"Fuck, I can't," he pants, sounding almost desperate. My hand rests against his throat, not putting any pressure on him, and I feel his Adam's apple bob against my palm as he swallows.

"Close your eyes, baby. Focus," I instruct him as I change the angle of my thrusts again, coming at his prostate straight on and making sure to drag against it on both the thrust and the outstroke, catching him both ways.

"Charlie, fuck, just… oh god." I feel him give up his resistance finally and slump against me, giving over to the pleasure and just letting himself experience it.

"That's it. Let me have you. All of you," I purr against his cheek, pressing kisses to every inch of his face and neck I can reach.

He whimpers as I wrap the hand not on his throat around his cock and start stroking him in time with my thrusts into his body, keeping him pinned against me as I work him over.

"That's right, baby. I've got you. Don't fight it. Let me take care of you."

"So. Good. So close…"

I pick up my pace, my hips hammering into him relentlessly as I work him with my fist, driving us both toward the edge. As much as I was enjoying dragging things out, I know I won't be able to hold on much longer.

"Fuck, you're so fucking tight, baby," I groan against his ear as I feel him start to tighten and pulse around me, his orgasm holding on by a thread. "So perfect. Gonna come for me?"

"God yeah, oh god," he pleads, and I can feel every muscle in his body start to tense, knowing he's right there, waiting for that final push.

"Do it," I growl. "Come for me, beautiful."

"Ah, fuck, Charlie, yes!" And with that, he comes on a scream, his hole clamping down almost painfully around my cock, triggering my own release. I continue my thrusts and work him with my fist, dragging every ounce out of our orgasms possible. At some point, one or both of our legs must have given out because the next thing I know, we are in a heap on my entryway floor, his spend splattered against the wall, and the man himself curled into my lap and resting on my chest while I sit back against a kitchen cabinet.

"Fuck, I needed that," Callum mumbles groggily against my chest.

"Me too," I say with a sigh, wrapping my arms around him, pulling him closer, and resting my cheek against his hair, a smile on my lips. We're both spent and barely able to catch our breath, but that was hands down the most intense experience of my life.

I've never been one for deep reflection or sweeping declarations. Still, as I feel Callum's breaths even out against my chest, I can't shake the feeling that my entire world just changed again.

CHAPTER TWENTY

CALLUM

*A*fter another bedtime consisting of two bathroom breaks, three glasses of water, three stories, and at least seven attempts at additional stalling, Georgie is finally down for the night. I collapse onto the couch, beer in hand, and let out a sigh of relief. My muscles ache from a long day at work and then chasing Georgie around for a few hours before bed, and all I want to do is kick back with a cold one and forget about the world. Charlie is closing tonight without me for once, so it's the first time I have been alone in weeks. I can't deny it's a little weird. I hadn't realized how used to having Charlie as part of our routine until tonight, when his absence felt like a glaring void.

As I sink into the cushions, my phone buzzes on the coffee table, and I see my sister Sarah's name flashing on the screen. With a grin, I answer, "Hey, sis, what's up?"

"Hey, Cal." Her cheerful voice comes through the line, hitting me with an unexpected pang of homesickness. "Just checking in. How's life treating my favorite brother?"

"Favorite, huh? Pretty sure I'm your only brother, but I'll take it," I chuckle. "Well, life's been… eventful." I launch into the cliff notes version of the last few weeks, catching her up on everything going on with Georgie, me, and the brewery. Sarah's laughter rings down the line, and I forget about the weight on my shoulders for a moment. But as the conversation winds down, I can't avoid the topic that's been gnawing at me.

"So, how's Charlie?" Sarah asks like she can read my mind.

"Charlie is…" I pause, searching for the right words. "Charlie is amazing, really. Things are good, you know?"

"Uh-oh, sounds like a 'but' coming on," she teases.

I run a hand through my hair, feeling suddenly vulnerable. "Yeah, but… I'm worried, Sarah. Worried that maybe I'm letting myself get too involved," I try to explain.

"What? Is it the 'he was straight a month ago' thing? You, of all people, should know better than most that sexuality is not only a spectrum but is fluid and can change," she says, her tone scolding and almost disappointed.

"Damn, Sarah. Have at least a little faith in me, yeah? Of course, it's not that. Yeah, it was a concern early on, but we worked past that, and let's just say that's definitely not an issue anymore."

Sarah makes an exaggerated gagging noise, and I can't hold back my laugh. "Ew. So don't need the details."

"You asked," I say with a shrug.

"I so did not. But stop stalling. What's the real issue here?"

I should know better than to try to distract her by now. She's like a shark sensing blood in the water, and there's no distracting her once she hones in on an issue. I let out a heavy sigh, feeling the weight of my concerns settle in my chest.

"It's good, Sarah. Really good. But I can't shake this feeling, you know? Like I'm standing on the edge of a cliff, and if I jump, I might lose something I can't get back. You know

Georgie is my top priority, and I can't help but worry that if I let myself make that jump, I'll be taking something away from her."

There's a thoughtful silence on the other end of the line before Sarah responds, her tone gentle. "Callum, you're an amazing dad. You've been holding down the fort for Georgie since day one. Being with someone doesn't take that away from you. You can be in love and be the fantastic father Georgie deserves. It's not one or the other."

"I know, I know. It's just… What if I mess this up?" I ask, my voice catching on the emotion threatening to clog my throat and choke me. "Georgie's been through so much already; I can't bear the thought of hurting her."

Sarah's tone becomes more serious as she responds. "Callum, you can't live your life in fear. You deserve happiness, too. And as sweet as she is, Georgie will benefit from seeing her dad happy and in love. You're not taking anything away from her; you're giving her a better life."

I sigh, feeling the weight of her words sink in. "I just can't help but worry, you know?"

"Of course you do, because you are an amazing father, Callum. You wouldn't worry so much if you didn't care." Sarah pauses, the air heavy between us for a moment. "You aren't them, Cal. Your love isn't a finite resource," she says, barely above a whisper.

Her words hit their mark, cutting through all the layers of bullshit I have built up around myself and nailing me straight in the heart. Neither of us talks about our parents often, and when we do, it's always in broad strokes or small shared memories, the few of those we have. They were a perfect example of two people doomed from the start. The duty-bound soldier and career-obsessed wife left behind when he went on deployments for years at a time before just not coming home from one at all. They claimed to love each other fiercely, but that fierceness often presents as volatility more than any level of real affection. They never should have had kids, but tried using us as a bandaid, something to keep them together. But when Dad was killed overseas, Mom checked out. Sarah and I were passed around various family members' houses before finally settling at our grandmothers when I was just starting High School and Sarah was about to graduate. If there is one lesson a kid in that situation learns, it's that love isn't enough, or there just isn't enough of it to go around.

So why would I risk Georgie like that? It just doesn't make sense. I'd rather cut my own heart out with a rusty blade than ever hurt her or have her wonder if there is enough room in my love and my life for her.

"I'm sorry, Cal. I know you don't like hearing that, but it's true," Sarah says, her voice soft and soothing, like she knows exactly how much she just made me bleed. "You don't have to make that decision now, Callum. Just take it one step at a time. You're an amazing father, and you deserve to be happy. Charlie seems like a good guy. Trust yourself; trust your instincts more than your memories. And most importantly, trust love."

"I'm not sure I believe in love," I admit, my voice finally breaking, matching the crack I feel tearing through my heart and the walls I've spent so many years building so carefully around it.

"Maybe you don't yet," she says, "but that doesn't mean it's not real. You're still healing, Cal. Don't rush it. Love has a funny way of finding us when we least expect it."

I sigh again, leaning back into the couch cushions. "Thanks, Sarah," I say, dragging a hand down over my face, trying to wipe the emotions away. "I needed to hear that."

"Anytime, little brother. Now, go have a good night, and give my love to Georgie. And, you know, Charlie, too."

I roll my eyes, a smile tugging at the corner of my lips. "Sure thing, sis. Talk to you later."

As I hang up, I'm left alone with my thoughts. The room is silent, and the ever-present weight on my shoulders feels a little lighter. Maybe Sarah's right. Maybe I can have it all—a relationship with Charlie and still be the dad I want to be for Georgie. But as I contemplate my sister's words and think back over the last few weeks, I'm hit with a realization.

This isn't something I need to try to solve, or even work on figuring out how to make it work... because it's already happening. Bedtime tonight was all the example I needed of the fact that I can be what Georgie needs and still have Charlie and get what I need, too. We keenly felt his absence tonight, Georgie even asking if she could call him to say goodnight on his break before she would settle in fully for the night.

The journey ahead might be challenging, but maybe, just maybe, it'll be worth it.

CHAPTER TWENTY-ONE

CHARLIE

*D*inner with my family is like stepping into a sitcom. There's a laugh track playing in the background of my mind as I navigate through the chaos of Alfie and Donnie arguing over the last bread roll, and Ollie and Georgie plotting covert operations to steal the other two bonehead's desserts while they aren't looking. But in the midst of this orchestrated chaos, there's a warmth, a sense of belonging that I'm immensely grateful I get to share with Callum and Georgie.

They sit at the table, blending seamlessly into my family. My mom fusses over Georgie, who giggles as she plays with her mashed potatoes, turning them into a mini mountain range. My dad, ever the storyteller, has Callum engaged in a story about all of us boys and the shit we used to get up to as kids, much to all of our collective embarrassment.

I catch Callum's eye across the table, and he shoots me a grateful smile. Despite the initial awkwardness with my brothers when he first moved to town, tonight feels like a turning point. The Larson's are a notoriously warm and welcoming lot, and it's easy to see Callum and Georgie have already been adopted into the crazy mess we call a family.

Dinner is a chaotic mess of conversation, with occasional bouts of laughter rising above the din of the voices and clatter of silverware against plates. My mom insists on refilling everyone's plates, and even though Callum tries to politely decline, she waves him off with a cheerful, "Nonsense, dear. You're family now."

Callum glances at me, a look I can't quite read behind his eyes, and I give him an encouraging nod. "Mom's right. You both are officially part of the Larson clan now," I say, raising my glass in a mock toast. He chuckles nervously. I can tell he's still not entirely used to the idea.

As dinner goes on, Callum starts to relax, joining in on the family banter and sharing a few stories of his own. Georgie's animated storytelling about her day at school brings a smile to everyone's face. I catch Callum stealing glances at me every so often, making me smile. There's a warmth in his eyes that wasn't there before, a kind of silent gratitude. It's as if he's finally realizing my family is embracing both him and Georgie with open arms.

We're halfway through dessert—fresh-baked cookies my mom and Georgie spent the afternoon making together—when I notice Georgie eyeing me curiously. Her big, innocent eyes meet mine, and I can't help but wonder what's going on in that imaginative little mind of hers.

"What's up, Georgie?" I ask.

She takes a moment, sizing me up before a grin spreads across her face. "Charles, I've been thinking."

"Oh, is that so, George? Should I be worried?" I tease.

She shakes her head, pigtails bouncing. "No, silly. I was just thinking... I think I'd be okay if you were my new Double Daddy."

Silence falls over the table. My mom, who was mid-sentence, freezes with a cookie halfway to her mouth. I can feel everyone's eyes on me, waiting for a response.

I resist glancing at Callum, not sure I am ready to face what I will find when I look at him, and wanting to keep this moment between Georgie and me.

"You know, sweetie," I say, grinning at Georgie, "I think I'd be okay with that too.

Callum nearly chokes on his bite of cookie, and I pat him on the back, suppressing a laugh. The rest of the family erupts into laughter, too, and the tension dissipates. Before I can enjoy the moment, though, Callum is on high alert when I finally look over at him. His eyes are wide, and he shifts uncomfortably in his seat. It's as if Georgie's innocent declaration has triggered a full-scale emergency in his mind.

"I, uh, need to use the restroom," he stammers, practically leaping from his chair. "Excuse me."

And just like that, he's gone, leaving behind a room full of bewildered Larsons, none more so than me. I can feel the annoyance and confusion building within me as I stare after him. Georgie's comment was innocent, but clearly, Callum is freaking out.

As the minutes tick by, and there's still no sign of Callum, my family begins to exchange concerned glances.

Georgie leans close from her seat next to me, tugging at my sleeve to get my attention. "Did I do something wrong?"

I shake my head, my heart breaking at the scared and sad look in her big blue eyes, and I offer her a reassuring smile, wrapping an arm around her shoulders and pulling her into my side for a hug. "No, sweetheart. Everything's fine. Your daddy just needs a minute."

But deep down, I can't shake the feeling that this moment might be more significant than any of us realize. Something has shifted, and I'm determined to figure out what's going on in Callum's head.

Excusing myself from the table, I head down the hall toward the bathroom, hoping to find Callum and offer him some reassurance. I knock on the door, but there's no response. Growing more concerned, I push it open to find Callum hastily splashing water on his face.

"Cal? What's going on?" I ask, my voice soft.

He startles at my voice, his eyes wide and panicked. "Nothing. Just needed some air."

I raise an eyebrow. "In the bathroom?"

He glances around the small space as if searching for an escape route. "Look, Charlie, I appreciate your family and everything, but this… it's too much too soon. I can't do the whole 'Double Daddy' thing. I need to go."

I'm taken aback by his sudden determination to escape. "Callum, wait. Georgie was just being cute. You know how kids are."

But he's already slipping past me, avoiding eye contact. "I can't, Charlie. I have to go."

And with that, he rushes back to the dining room to scoop up Georgie and make his excuses before disappearing out the front door, leaving me standing there, utterly confused and more than a little pissed.

What just happened?

CHAPTER TWENTY-TWO

CALLUM

A week after the amazing and disastrous dinner with Charlie's family, the annual Oktoberfest party is in full swing at Spirit of Hops. The parking lot between the brewery and Valkyrie bar has been closed off, and our patio expanded to take up the entire space with additional tables and room for a handful of cornhole boards. Three different food trucks are lined up along the curb, each with their own take on the traditional German fare you'd expect to see at an Oktoberfest celebration. The air is thick with the scent of sizzling bratwurst and the rich aroma of freshly brewed beer. It's the kind of festive atmosphere that should make anyone's heart light, but for me, it's more like navigating a minefield.

I've been successfully avoiding Charlie all week, convinced that Georgie's innocent but nerve-wracking 'Double Daddy' incident was enough to scare him off. I've been dodging him like a pro, making excuses like extra inventory checks at work and feigning illness or drama with my sister to miss him outside of our shared shifts.

It's absolutely the most chicken-shit move I have ever pulled, and I hate myself for doing it, but that scared, broken part of me that is always convinced the people around me are going to leave got the better of me and decided I should leave first before he has a chance to hurt me. Fuck, he has every right to kick my ass for this bullshit. But apparently, on top of being chicken-shit, I am also an absolute coward because it took about 2.5 seconds after gathering Georgie up and hustling her out of Charlie's parents' house after that dinner for me to realize the giant mistake I was making… but have I sucked it up and done anything about it? Of course not. So here I am, six days later, skirting the edges of the brewery's celebration, trying my best to stay out of Charlie's line of sight. Every time I catch a glimpse of his tousled hair or the way his eyes light up when he laughs with a customer, my resolve weakens.

It's not that I truly want to avoid him or never see him again. It's the absolute opposite. I've been bracing myself for the inevitable conversation, the one where he tells me he's not ready to be a part of this mess I call a life. The one where he admits that my adorable, precocious daughter might be more than he bargained for. I'm convinced that any moment now, Charlie will corner me and end whatever we had been building together.

And the worst part is, I don't know that I would blame him. I'm a lot, *we're* a lot, especially for a man who never really considered kids before diving into this thing with me. He went from being a carefree single ladies' man who enjoyed flirting and playing the field when he felt like it, to being in a relationship with a man and playing stepdad to that man's handful of a six-year-old daughter. It's a lot for anyone to take on, and I wouldn't blame him for saying it's too much. It would fucking kill me, but I'd understand.

As the afternoon wears on into evening and the party picks up, I wind up stuck pulling pints behind the bar and putting on my best fake smile for the customers, my eyes continually scanning the room for any sign of Charlie. It's weird, I would have expected to be here today, even if just to hang out with his brothers and friends, if not working.

The taproom is packed by now, and the cheerful hum of conversation makes it easy to miss the subtle shifting of the crowd. Without notice, the lights dim, and the buzz of excitement swells through the room.

I glance toward the makeshift stage set up in the far corner of the taproom for tonight, where a couple of local bands have been playing all day, and there will be karaoke later, I think. The mass of string lights Emily and Lottie strung up over the stage turns back on, casting a soft, warm glow over the small platform. And there he is. With his tousled blond hair and infectious grin, Charlie stands tall with a guitar slung over his shoulder. Did I know he could play the guitar? Of course, the man can play. He's good at just about everything.

Charlie clears his throat, and the room falls almost silent, all eyes on him. "Hey, everyone!" he says, stepping up to the microphone and adjusting the stand slightly. "I hope you're all having an awesome time at Spirit of Hops annual Okto-berfest!"

The crowd erupts in cheers, clinking glasses and raising them in salute.

"To make this night even more unforgettable," Charlie continues, "I'd like to dedicate a song to a certain someone special."

My heart skips a beat. Could he possibly be talking about me? I glance around nervously, but Charlie's gaze is locked on mine. I swallow hard, my throat suddenly dry.

"Here's the answer to a question he's been too afraid to ask," Charlie says with a smirk, shooting me a wink as he strums a couple chords on the guitar to settle in before plucking out the unmistakable opening notes of a song any respectable Millennial sang their hearts out to entirely too many years ago now. He's playing a softer, more intimate acoustic version of Paramours "Still Into You," and I can't help but gasp.

The crowd murmurs in recognition, and Charlie starts to sing. His voice, a perfect blend of soulful and rough, wraps around the lyrics like a warm embrace. The sincerity in his eyes as he looks at me makes my heart race, and the brewery fades away, leaving just him and me.

When he gets to the second verse, I notice a slight change in the lyrics, making them mimic our actual experience of meeting his family instead of the other way around. I can feel tears pricking at the corners of my eyes as he pours his heart into the song. The realization hits me like a ton of bricks—he's not running away. He's declaring his feelings in front of damn near the whole town, and I can't help but be over-whelmed by the sheer audacity of his grand gesture.

As the last notes of the song linger in the air, the room erupts in applause. Charlie smiles, his eyes never leaving mine, and steps away from the mic. The crowd is still buzzing with excitement when he steps off the stage and starts walking through the sea of people, directly toward me.

I'm frozen in place behind the bar, vaguely aware of the other bartenders slipping away as my heart pounds in my ears. The distance between us closes, and I can see the genuine affection in his eyes. The background noise fades, and when he rounds the end of the bar, it's just the two of us.

Without saying a word, he closes the remaining distance, cups my face in his hands, and presses his lips to mine. The world stops, and it's just us, lost in the heartbreaking sweet-ness and warmth of this kiss. The crowd's cheers become distant echoes as our connection deepens, a silent affirma-tion of the feelings that words can't convey.

When we finally break the kiss, Charlie rests his forehead

against mine, his breath mingling with mine. "I'm still into you, Callum Bowers," he whispers, his voice filled with sincerity, his thumb gently brushing against my cheek.

The weight I've been carrying around for longer than I can remember lifts from my chest, and I feel like I can take my first deep breath in years, a fresh set of tears pricking my eyes as I gasp out a strange, choked mix of a sob and a laugh. I've been so afraid of letting someone in, afraid of being hurt again, that I almost missed my chance with this amazing man. But here he is, standing in front of me, laying his heart bare.

Snaking my hands around his waist, I tug him just a bit closer and finally say the words my heart has been screaming at me almost since the day this man literally crashed into my life, but I was simply stubborn to admit. "I'm still into you, too, Charlie Larson."

His eyes drop closed, and I feel him let out a breath, his whole body sagging in relief at my words. He braces like that for a moment before responding, our foreheads still pressed together, enjoying the little bubble we have created for ourselves in this moment. "Good. I want to be in it with you, with both you and Georgie, all in, for as long as you'll have me."

My fingers flex against his lower back, and I smile at his declaration of intention and the fact that I want nothing more than exactly that. "Better settle in then, forever can be a very hoppy long time," I say, internally cringing at my horrible fumble of an attempt at a beer-related pun, but when he stares at me wide-eyed, his face all but split in two with a giant grin I know I've hit my mark.

With a laugh, Charlie tosses his head back and hollers to the rafters, "PUN-NY JAR!" before stealing my breath with another knee-weakening kiss.

Yeah, I am so still into this man.

CHAPTER TWENTY-THREE

CHARLIE

He wants me. He wants me to stay. I can't say I ever really doubted otherwise, but having a good feeling about something and actually hearing the words come out of the other person's mouth as you're wrapped in their arms is on a completely different level.

The echo of applause and cheers from the crowd still rings in my ears as Callum and I step out from behind the bar, our fingers tightly interwoven. I glance at Callum; his eyes lit up like a neon sign, and a goofy grin on his face that mirrors mine. The grand romantic gesture my family had all demanded I make after Callum ran scared after dinner last week worked. The heartfelt song with lyrics that couldn't be more perfect—I'd put myself out there, and Callum reciprocated in a way I never imagined. I'd hoped, for sure, but I never let myself believe I would be lucky enough to win him over. My expert Kool-Aid man bursting through walls skills be damned.

It's been a week of sleepless nights, stomach-churning anxiety, and an extreme excess of coffee. Callum spent the week avoiding me at all costs, nervous glances and the way he fumbled his words, telling me more than words ever could. He was scared, afraid of what admitting his feelings for me could mean. I can't blame him, not with Georgie to consider. But I couldn't let that fear hold us back.

So, I planned this surprise, enlisted the help of my brothers and a couple other people from the Brewery staff, and took center stage to declare my feelings in the most public way possible. Now, as we walk through the crowd of what I am pretty sure is every single resident of Rapids Bay, I can't help but replay the night events in my mind. The fear of rejection, the anticipation, the way I was absolutely convinced I would get up there and completely forget how to play guitar even though I've been playing since elementary school. And finally, the overwhelming joy as I finally wrapped Callum in my arms again.

We try to hang around for a bit, making our way around the taproom to say our hellos and thank you's to the people who made this happen, but the swarm of congratulations quickly becomes too much. A sea of familiar faces and strangers alike descends upon us, offering hugs, clinks of their glasses, and hearty cheers. My mom squeezes through the crowd at some point and gives us each a tight hug before waving us off with a knowing smile. She's already texted, letting us know she'll take Georgie back to my parent's place tonight for a sleepover. It's like she's been waiting for this moment almost as eagerly as I have.

"Cal," I lean in, my voice a soft murmur against his ear. "Let's get out of here before we suffocate under all these well-wishers."

He nods, his eyes filled with gratitude. We slip away from the chaos, beating a stealthy retreat through the back door, careful not to attract attention. The night air is crisp, a welcome contrast to the warmth and closeness of the packed taproom. As we breathe a shared sigh of relief, I can feel the weight of the week lifting from my shoulders. We did it. We faced our fears, took the plunge, and came out the other side, still holding hands. I'm sure there are some other cliches I can throw in there, too, but I'm just too happy to care at this point.

"Barbie's got Georgie covered for the night," I say, unsure if he's seen the text.

His eyes light up with a mix of surprise and gratitude. "She did that for us?"

I chuckle, "She's doing it, babe. My mother is a force to be reckoned with. She's been shipping us harder than anyone else in town, so if she can help get us together in any way, you bet your sweet ass she'll do it."

We share a laugh, the tension of the past week finally dissipating. With a glance at each other, we reach the unspoken agreement to head to Callum's apartment, which has quickly become our home base over the last few weeks. We both need a quiet refuge from the chaos we just left inside the brewery.

The drive to Callum's apartment is quiet, the engine's hum and the radio's steady beat filling the space between us. I steal glances at him, watching the way the streetlights reflect in his eyes. He seems more relaxed than I have seen him up to this point, the tension that has gripped him for as long as I've known him slowly melting away.

When we step into his apartment, the air is thick between us with anticipation. Callum runs a hand through his hair, looking both relieved and content. "I can't believe you did that. Singing in front of everyone? That was..." his words trail off as he smiles at me.

I grin, feeling a sense of accomplishment. "Sometimes you have to go big or go home, right?"

Cal chuckles, pulling me into a comforting hug. "You certainly went big. I never expected something like that."

"I just wanted to show you how much you mean to me, Cal. And it worked, didn't it? I say, my voice a mix of playfulness and sincerity.

He looks at me, those hazel eyes filled with a depth of emotion that tugs at my heartstrings. "It definitely worked. I never thought I'd find someone like you."

I raise an eyebrow. "Someone crazy enough to make a fool of himself in front of a whole town just to prove he's not going anywhere?"

"Exactly. Crazy in the best way," he replies, his smile lighting up my soul.

I pull him in for another hug, needing to just hold him after everything. I swear my intentions were pure, but it doesn't take long for air to shift around us, the tension ramping up with the subtle shift of our hips against each other, the flexing of my fingers against his neck where I hold him to my chest, and the shifting of his grip at my lower back from a press to gripping the hem of my shirt in his fist.

"So…" I rasp, my voice rough with sudden desire as I drag out the word. "Movies and cuddling, yeah?" I say with a wicked smirk.

Callum crushes his lips to mine without missing a beat, nipping at my bottom lip before pulling back just enough to growl, "Later," into the kiss.

I don't need to be told twice. When I see his eyes darken and hear this voice drop to that sexy lower register he only gets when thoroughly aroused, I know exactly what's coming.

We stumble down the hallway to his room, lips and hands never leaving the other person for longer than necessary as we tear at each other's clothes, fumbling and grasping for skin wherever we can manage to uncover it. We tumble through the doorway and kick it closed behind us. His hands grip my waist and pull me closer. I can feel him hard against me, already wanting me.

"Mmm," I moan. "Missed you, baby."

"Missed you, too."

"God, you're killing me," I breathe, breaking the kiss long enough to pull Callum's shirt over his head and throw it across the room. "So sexy."

Callum groans, shaking his head in denial. "No. You. So fucking gorgeous."

I chuckle. "Flattery will get you everywhere."

"Good," he replies, nipping at my bottom lip before sweeping his tongue out to soothe over the spot.

Something about that move has my reserve snapping. I growl, sinking my hands into Callum's hair and dragging him close, crushing our lips together.

"Get on the bed."

"Yessir," he says with a wink, pulling away and sauntering over to climb onto the mattress.

I quickly strip off the remnants of my clothing, leaving my boxers in place for now, knowing I need that little bit of barrier if I want to make this last the way I want it to. My eyes scan the bed, and the sight before me has my brain short-circuiting and my mouth running dry.

Callum, shirtless, is kneeling in the center of the bed, hands resting on his thighs and dick straining against his jeans. The bulge is thick and hard, and just begging me to set it free. A thrill shoots down my spine, and I can't help the low groan that slips from my lips.

"You're so beautiful."

"So are you."

I smile, moving closer and climbing onto the bed. Kneeling in front of him, I run my hands slowly over his muscular chest, reveling in the feel of taut muscle and the tickle of coarse hair against my palms. My thumbs graze across his hardened nipples and then slide higher, cupping his jaw and pulling him into a deep kiss.

Without breaking our connection, I guide Callum backward, urging him to scoot back until he can lie back and rest against the pillows. He pulls back to adjust and finds a comfortable spot, watching as I straddle him and continue my slow, gentle touches. I lean forward again, and our kisses start out slow, almost chaste, but grow more passionate by the second as I continue my exploration of his body. Tongues duel, and teeth nip gently, sending waves of pleasure and passion rippling between us.

"God, you're perfect," I whisper against his neck, kissing and licking at the skin there, teasing him the way I know he likes it.

Callum hums in contentment at my words, his hands roaming my body, caressing anything he can reach. We've been together enough times now; we know all the little places on each other's bodies to drive the other crazy. With gentle fingers, we both exercise that knowledge, exploring each other's flesh, rubbing and caressing, and enjoying the sounds we can pull from the other.

Eventually, I break the kiss, sitting up and reaching for the bottle of lube and a condom from the nightstand. When I don't move from my position, straddling his hips as I pop open the lube, he raises an eyebrow at me in question. "What are you doing?"

"Thought I'd ride you tonight," I state, tossing the supplies onto the mattress next to his shoulder.

Callum's jaw drops. "Really? You want to bottom for me? Like, for real?" We've teased and joked about it before, but I've never actually done it. Tonight just feels right as the time to take that step.

"Yeah," I whisper. "I do. If you'll have me."

"Are you kidding? Of course I want you. I crave any part of you that you're willing to give."

I lean forward and press another kiss to his lips before reaching for the lube again.

"You sure?" he asks, and if I didn't know him better, I would say he was trying to talk me out of it, but I know his hesitancy is from a place of caring and making sure I truly want this.

"It's you. I want everything with you."

Callum smiles at my answer and quickly rolls, reversing our position and laying me out on the mattress beneath him.

"Then allow me," he says with a smirk.

He kisses me again, our tongues tangling and bodies pressing together. My hips lift off the bed, grinding our cocks together and creating a delicious friction. Callum breaks the kiss and trails his lips down my neck. As his tongue swirls around my left nipple, his hand rubs over the bulge in my boxers, ripping a moan from me.

"Like that, sir?" he purrs against my skin, his teeth raking across my nipple and sending bolts of heat straight to my balls. Not to mention the cheeky bastard "sir-ing" me. I've never been one for roleplay or honorifics, but fuck if that word from him doesn't do something to me.

"Y-yes," I pant in answer to his question.

"What about this?" He makes quick work of tugging my boxers down my thighs and helping me kick them off, sending them flying across the room somewhere. When he returns to my cock, my erection hot and throbbing and waiting for him, he glides his palm over the shaft, just grazing against it but offering no real friction.

"Fuck!" I gasp, my hips bucking and breath hitching.

Cal chuckles. "Well, that's the idea, alright."

His fingers wrap around my shaft, stroking it from root

to tip and clearly enjoying the way he's making me squirm if his smirk is anything to go by.

"God, please," I whimper.

Callum releases my cock and pulls back. He takes a moment to shuck his jeans and boxers as well, tossing them over his shoulder as his attention returns to me.

"Mmm, look at that," he murmurs.

"Don't tease," I beg.

Cal grins and leans down, placing a soft kiss on the head of my cock. "Wouldn't dream of it."

The tip of his tongue darts out and circles the head, before opening wide and taking me deep with one long swallow. I groan and thrust up, forcing my cock into his throat. Cal bobs over me, sucking hard. His mouth moves, taking the length before pulling back and running his tongue along the underside, toying with me.

"Fuck, Cal," I moan.

Cal just grins before sucking back to the root and swallowing.

"Fuuuuck," I hiss, dragging it out as I savor the feel of his throat rippling around me.

Callum swallows again before begging to move, his head riding and falling, working me over. His cheeks are hollow, and his throat muscles work to accommodate the intrusion. I lose track of everything but the feel of his mouth around me, and I can't imagine what kinds of sounds he's pulling from me.

I feel my orgasm start to build, and I push against his shoulder. "Stop. Not like this," I rasp, barely able to string those few words together.

Callum pulls back, letting my spit-covered erection slip from his mouth with an obscene pop.

"Fuck me, please," I beg, meeting his eyes, seeing the heat and need I am feeling reflected back in his.

"Anything you want," he replies, reaching for the lube and popping the cap, coating his fingers. I spread my legs for him, accommodating him as he settles on his knees between my thighs. He reaches forward, a look of utterly adorable concentration furrowing his brow as he circles the puckered opening with one finger before pushing inside.

"Yes," I sigh.

Callum twists and turns the digit, pressing further in little by little with each movement before adding a second. He scissors his fingers inside me, stretching the tight muscles, and then a third.

"Oh, God," I groan, my head rolling and my hips pushing against his invading fingers.

"You good?" he asks, his smirk evident in his voice, even though I can't manage to open my eyes to look at him.

"So fucking good."

"Ready for my cock?"

"Yes. Yes, please," I say, prying my eyes open to meet his. "How do you want me?" I ask, panting.

"Exactly like this. Want to touch you, watch your eyes roll back as I fill you," Callum says, pressing tender kisses along my jaw and upper chest as he continues the motion of his fingers. My body wracks with shivers, and all I can manage is a hummed ascent to his words, already feeling myself be swept away by the pleasure and intensity of his ministrations.

Callum smiles and kisses his way back to my lips, taking them in a fierce, passionate kiss. When the kiss ends, and he pulls back, I look down and see he's already slipped on the condom and is holding his cock, guiding it toward my stretched and waiting hole. He helps me lift my legs, knees splayed wide to offer him a better angel and all but coos, "Relax for me."

I take a deep breath and do my best to relax, remembering the words I've said to him countless times while our positions have been reversed... remember to breathe and push back against him. The pressure of his thick head penetrating me is intense and sends a shiver down my spine.

"Oh, fuck," I groan.

"Too much?" Callum asks, holding still and giving me a moment to adjust.

"Perfect," I say with a sigh, relishing the stretch and burn of his invasion.

Once fully seated to the hilt, Callum stills, letting my muscles adjust again, his hands trailing over the backs of my thighs and chest in an effort to distract me. After a minute, I rock my hips against him experimentally.

"Oh, fuck me," I curse, the feeling of him moving inside me like nothing I could have imagined.

"Your wish is my command," he says, intentionally misconstruing my words, starting at a slow, steady pace.

Needing something to hold on to and desperate to have him close, I wrap my arms around his back, reaching up toward his shoulders to press him closer. Our lips connect in a searing kiss, tongues and teeth clashing. As the speed and intensity of Callum's thrusts increase, my back arches, and I dig my nails into the smooth skin of his strong back.

"Oh, yes, God," I groan.

Callum gasps in pleasure above me, his hips pistoning. "Fuck, so fucking perfect," he cries out. "So fucking tight for me."

"Baby, I'm not going to last," I whimper.

"Neither am I. Come with me," he urges, reaching between us and wrapping his fist around my neglected cock, pumping me in time with his thrusts.

"Yes! Oh, fuck, Cal, I'm..."

"That's it, come for me," he growls, his thrusts coming harder and faster.

A moment later, my cum shoots over his fist as I feel him swell in my ass, his own release barreling through him as his hips lose their rhythm. My hole clenches around him as I cum, pushing him over the edge with me.

"Fuck, baby, I'm coming," I say unnecessarily as my body convulses, and I swear I see stars.

"Give it to me," he grunts, slamming home a few more times as his cock twitches, filling the condom before he collapses across my chest, his pleasant weight pressing me into the mattress, and I struggle to catch my breath.

"Shit. Sorry," he pants when he notices my struggle.

"It's fine," I say, wrapping my arms around him and holding him close, unwilling to let him go just yet.

"You okay?" Callum asks, genuine care and concern in his voice.

"Mmmhmm," I hum. Callum chuckles, placing gentle kisses on my sweaty forehead.

"Love you," I whisper, my eyes drifting closed as sleep beckons me under.

A second later, every last muscle in my body goes rigid, and my eyes fly open, realizing what I just said. We haven't exchanged those particular words before, and tonight was intense enough as it was. The last thing I want is to scare him off now by coming on too strong all at once, not when I finally have him.

Cal chuckles at my reaction, leaning in to press a soft, lingering kiss against my lips. "I love you, too," he says into the kiss.

"You don't have to say it just because I did," I say, trying to reassure him I didn't mean to pressure him.

He pulls back, bracing his elbows on the bed by my shoulders so we can focus and look at each other. "I'm not. I mean it."

The admission hangs in the air, a tangible declaration that

solidifies the connection between us. It's a simple phrase, but the weight it carries is monumental. We've laid our hearts bare to one another for the first time, and the honesty is liberating.

"Thank you," is all I say, my eyes softening as I look up at him, and I hope he can see everything I wish I could find words for in them.

"For what?" he asks, pressing a kiss to the tip of my nose.

"Trusting me."

Callum smiles and lays his head on my shoulder. "Always."

CHAPTER TWENTY-FOUR

CALLUM

The morning sun peeks through the blinds, casting a warm glow across the room. I blink my eyes open, momentarily disoriented by the light and feel of something warm and solid behind me. Then it all comes rushing back—the grand gesture, the support and love of the people we care about most, the kisses that turned into lovemaking, and the fact that I'm tangled up in Charlie's arms.

I crane my neck to look over my shoulder at his peaceful face as he sleeps wrapped around me, snoring softly, and can't help but smile. I could absolutely get used to waking up like this. Feeling the call of nature, I gently extricate myself from the tangle of sheets and stumble to the bathroom to take care of business before making my way to the kitchen, the scent of coffee already wafting through the air from the automatic coffee maker Charlie brought over a few days after the first night he spent here, claiming my machine just wasn't good enough for his discerning tastes.

Charlie stumbles into the kitchen, still half-asleep but wearing that adorably disheveled look that makes my heart skip a beat. "Morning, handsome," I greet him with a grin.

"Morning," he mumbles, his eyes barely open. He shuffles over and wraps his arms around my waist, resting his head on my shoulder. "This is nice."

"Mmm," I hum in agreement, reveling in the warmth of his body against mine as we settle into what feels dangerously close to a morning routine.

"I could get used to this," I say, pouring him a mug as he peppers soft kisses along my shoulder.

"What, having me here in the morning? Or my highly superior coffee?" he teases, nipping my ear lightly.

"The coffee, obviously," I deadpan.

We spend the morning in a lazy haze, sipping coffee and talking about last night, swapping stories of what we missed in the previous week apart, and plans for the upcoming week. There's a comfort in the easy way we fit together, like puzzle pieces finding their place.

Eventually, Charlie suggests we go pick up Georgie from his parents' house. "She probably thinks we abandoned her or something," he says with a chuckle.

As much as I have enjoyed this quiet time together, I am ready to see my little monster again. It doesn't take us long to shower and get ready for the day. It's amazing how quickly we can manage it when Charlie promises to keep his hands to himself. It lets me get him off so much more quickly without him interfering.

When we pull up to the Larson's house, Barbie and Joel welcome me with open arms. I get more hugs than I've had in years, and it feels like I have found something I've never had before: a real, loving family. It's overwhelming in the best possible way.

Brunch is lively, filled with laughter and the clinking of cutlery. Georgie bounces in her seat, animatedly recounting her night with Charlie's parents. "Nana makes the best pancakes," she declares through a mouthful of syrupy goodness. "She and pop-pop taught me how to make them before you got here!"

"Nana and Pop-pop?" Charlie asks, shooting his parents a reproachful look. I'm sure he is worried about me freaking out again or thinking it's too soon. But the man doesn't realize that when I said I was all in last night, I meant all the way. I want Charlie and everything that comes with him, including his massive, loving, and slightly insane family.

After brunch, we head out for a day of fun, wanting to spend the day just the three of us. Charlie surprises us with a trip to the ice cream parlor—Georgie's eyes light up like it's Christmas morning. Once we are settled in a corner booth, each tucking into our ice cream, Georgie clears her throat, settling on her knees and giving us a serious look.

"Charles, Daddy, have something I want to talk to you both about," she begins.

Charlie and I exchange looks across the table, fighting to hide our laughter at her ridiculousness.

"Yes, George? What can we do for you?" Charlie asks, schooling his expression and matching her serious tone.

She looks between us, ensuring we are both focused on her, before declaring, "I think Charles should move in with us."

My eyes snap to Charlie's, unsure of just how freaked out he will be by this little declaration. Though, I really should know better by now. If the Double Daddy one didn't send him running, it shouldn't be a surprise when I see nothing but delight in those ice-blue eyes staring back at me.

"Oh, you think so, George?" Charlie asks, shooting me a wink.

"Uh-huh, I do. You make Daddy happy. He smiles more when you are around. And your jokes are funnier when Daddy is there to make fun of them. Oh, and Nana Barbie says you two make her heart happy. I like Nana Barbie, so I want her heart to be happy, too."

My jaw must be on the floor after that little speech. Where did my child learn to be such a master manipulator? I can't tell if I'm scared or impressed. I settle on impressed when I look over at Charlie and see him blink rapidly like he's fighting off his emotions.

"You really want him to be at our house all the time?" I ask.

She gives me a look like I am the dumbest human to ever walk the earth before saying, "Of course, Daddy. He's a better cook than you, too. He should move in."

"Well, can't argue with that logic," Charlie laughs.

"Georgie… I don't…" I start to say, but she cuts me off.

"Are you two boyfriends?" she asks.

Charlie and I share a smile across the table before he answers for us. "Yeah, sweetie, we are."

She sighs dramatically, putting a hand to her heart. "Finally! Well, it's settled then. You love each other, and people that are in love are supposed to live together."

With that, Georgie flops down on the seat and digs into her ice cream like the topic is settled and there's nothing else to discuss.

Charlie and I exchange amused glances before bursting into laughter. Georgie joins in, her giggles contagious.

Once our ice cream is finished, we leave the parlor, hands sticky, and sugar rushes in full effect. The sun is dipping in the sky as we make our way back to our apartment, Georgie skipping ahead, her excitement palpable.

As we enter the apartment, Georgie throws her arms wide, declaring, "Welcome home, Daddy and Charlie!"

Charlie looks at me with a mixture of surprise and affection. "Home, huh?" he whispers.

I nod, smiling. "Seems like it."

Georgie tugs on Charlie's hand, her eyes wide with anticipation. "So, you are moving in, right?"

Charlie sputters, caught off guard by her directness. He glances at me, silently pleading for help.

Georgie rolls her eyes and crosses her arms. "Well, obviously, you have to. I need my double daddy around all the time."

"Double daddy? You've said that before. What exactly does that mean, sweetie?" I ask, needing to finally figure out what she means by that.

She nods with all the seriousness a six-year-old can muster. "Yep, one for fun and one for serious stuff. Like, you can teach me how to play cards, and Daddy can help me with math homework."

I snort an offended laugh, ruffling her hair. "I can do fun stuff too, you know."

Georgie gives me a skeptical look. "We'll see about that. But for real… You're my Double Daddies now. We gotta stick together!"

Charlie looks at me, a silent question in his eyes. I just shrug, smiling. "Guess you're stuck with us, double daddy."

He laughs, pulling Georgie into a hug. "Stuck? Nah, this is the best kind of stuck I've ever been."

And just like that, our little family takes shape amid giggles and sticky fingers. The uncertainty of the future is replaced by the warmth of the present. As we settle into the evening, I can't help but feel grateful for this unexpected journey. With a double daddy, a pint-sized dictator, and the promise of many more lazy mornings, our story is just beginning.

EPILOGUE

CALLUM

The brewery is buzzing with laughter and the clinking of glasses as the first weekend of January unfolds. Charlie, the man who wears flannel like a fashion statement, orchestrates the celebration like a maestro. He's in his element, making sure all the moving pieces of the celebration come together. If he caught me looking, I'd have big dumb hearts in my eyes as I stare at him.

It's my big night — the release of my first solo brew. A dark honey ale that's smooth as silk, with a touch of sweetness that makes you want to savor every drop. It's not just a beer; it's a new beginning, a mix of things you wouldn't expect to work, but they come together to make something new, beautiful, and unique.

All Spirit of Hops and Valkyrie Bar employees are here to join the party. I wasn't expecting anything special, but Mac, Kendric, and Luka went all out for tonight. The brewery is filled with familiar faces and feels like one big, happy family. But one face stands out among the sea of smiles—Charlie's. His grin is as infectious as his laughter, and his eyes gleam with pride.

I take another swig of my pint, still marveling at how amazing it is that I actually did it.

Charlie looks at me with those piercing blue eyes and asks, "So, you gonna drink it or make love to it?"

My mouth drops open, and I can't decide if I'm more embarrassed or turned on. Smacking him lightly in the chest, I scold him to behave. I am so going to get him back for that later.

"Well, if I can't be naughty, how about you kiss me instead?" He winks.

He doesn't have to ask twice. Setting my pint down, I lean over and press my lips to his. It doesn't matter where we are or what we are doing; I will always kiss this man every chance I get.

"Get a room!" Mac calls out.

Pulling away, I smile at him and shake my head. We're surrounded by old and new friends, and this is the happiest I can remember being.

"Thanks, Mac. For everything," I say.

"Anytime, man. Anytime. Ready to say a few words?" he asks, not waiting for my response before clearing his throat loudly and hollering over the din of the crowd to get everyone's attention.

"Attention, everyone! It's time to thank the man of the hour for giving us all a taste of his sweet, sweet honey."

A few people laugh; others groan and shake their heads. Emily calls out, demanding a donation to the jar for that one. Rolling my eyes at Mac, I move to the stage in the corner and take a deep breath before starting my speech.

"Hey, everyone! Thanks for being here tonight. This beer, this beautiful dark honey ale, is my love letter to you all, this new town I am proud to call home. It's a little bit of magic, a dash of love, and a whole lot of inspiration. I owe it all to someone special." I raise my glass, and all eyes turn to Charlie.

The crowd erupts into cheers, and Charlie blushes, looking both proud and bashful. "To Charlie—the man who taught me that life is better with a hint of sweetness... and that damn pun-ny jar."

My eyes drift to Charlie, sitting on a barstool near the front, looking like a dream. My cheeks flush when I realize I've probably got the same goofy grin he's sporting.

"Now, without further ado, I'm excited to announce the newest addition to the brewery's lineup: Honey Sweet."

"Thank you, and enjoy," I call out before stepping down and making my way back to the man I love.

"I'm so proud of you, babe," Charlie whispers in my ear.

"I wouldn't have had the courage to try this without your encouragement."

"You would have found a way. You're fucking amazing. I love you. So damn much."

His eyes are misty and full of pride.

"And I love you."

We kiss, ignoring the cheers and hoots from the people around us. Right now, it's just the two of us, and that's all that matters.

As the glasses clink and the toasts are made, I feel a small tug on my jeans. I glance down to see Georgie looking up at me with wide, innocent eyes. She holds up a miniature plastic cup filled with apple juice.

"Daddy, you did good!" she declares, her face beaming with pride.

I bend down, ruffling her hair. "Thanks, sweetheart. Couldn't have done it without you and Charlie."

Georgie beams at the compliment, and I find myself looking at them both with a heart full of warmth. In this moment, surrounded by friends, laughter, and the lingering scent of honey ale, I realize something profound.

I have a family here. It's not the conventional kind, but it's real, filled with love, and it's mine. As Charlie, Georgie, and I stand together, toasting to the success of the brew and the joy of unexpected connections, I can't help but feel grateful for the sweet twist of fate that brought us all together. Our lives won't be simple, but there is one thing I know without a shadow of a doubt. They will be straight-up amazing.

The End

ACKNOWLEDGMENTS

First off, Jackie, my twin, my soul sister. Nothing about this book would have been possible without you. Not a single word would have gotten written if it weren't for your love, support, and borderline abusive (in the best way) brand of encouragement.

Kayla and Randee, you two round out our little group and the unwavering support and never-ending stream of weird gifs and memes give me life.

All my love to my amazing betas: Jackie, Gretchen, and Jes. I adore you all and watching you guys fall in love with these boys as much as I have makes everything worth it.

To K, my amazing cover designer, thank you for putting up with my last minute late night insanity when it came to this cover. You absolutely knocked it out of the park and I am obsessed with everything you do.

Last but certainly not least, to my wonderful hubster. Thank you for putting up with my scatterbrained ridiculousness when I get lost in a story, your support and understanding when it comes to giving me the space and ability to explore my passion, and for not citing the mountain of unwashed dishes in any future letters of complaint or divorce filings 😊 (Oh I'm only joking.. you're stuck with me forever mwhahahah)

ALSO BY J.E. JOYCE

Spirit of Hops Series

Love With A Twist - books2read.com/u/mB5KaO

Not So Straight Up - books2read.com/u/316Kj7

Standalones

Chasing Sunsets - books2read.com/u/4A2v8N

WITH JAYCEE WOLFE

UNGRATEFUL DEAD MC
Corpse: Ungrateful Dead MC Book - books2read.com/u/3nGYWB

HARPIES HOLLOW: MAYHEM COVEN
Hopeless Chaos - books2read.com/u/3yQkkn

STALK J.E. JOYCE

Website:
www.AuthorJEJoyce.com
Facebook:
https://www.facebook.com/j.e.joyce.author
Goodreads:
https://www.goodreads.com/author/show/24510228.
J_E_Joyce
Bookbub:
https://www.bookbub.com/authors/j-e-joyce
Instagram:
https://www.instagram.com/author.j.e.joyce/

ABOUT THE AUTHOR

J.E. Joyce lives in the frozen hellscape *cough* sorry, the lovely snow-covered dreamscape that is Minnesota. She is an unrepentant coffee addict, lifelong Broadway fanatic and theater geek, and thinks Deadpool absolutely counts as a chick flick. When she isn't melting pages with the steamy dreamy book boyfriends in her head, she's annoying the ever-loving heck outta her hubster and two mini monsters.